MAX MORGAN
THE SACRIFICE

SHELLEY MURPHY

Bloomington, IN Milton Keynes, UK

 authorHOUSE®

AuthorHouse™
1663 Liberty Drive, Suite 200
Bloomington, IN 47403
www.authorhouse.com
Phone: 1-800-839-8640

AuthorHouse™ UK Ltd.
500 Avebury Boulevard
Central Milton Keynes, MK9 2BE
www.authorhouse.co.uk
Phone: 08001974150

This book is a work of fiction. People, places, events, and situations are the product of the author's imagination. Any resemblance to actual persons, living or dead, or historical events, is purely coincidental.

First published by AuthorHouse 10/24/2006

ISBN: 1-4208-9649-0 (sc)
ISBN: 1-4208-9648-2 (dj)

Library of Congress Control Number: 2005909675

Printed in the United States of America
Bloomington, Indiana

This book is printed on acid-free paper.

For my son Markus, I know how you dislike reading, so I strived to write an adventure that would develop your interest in the written word. For my son Mason, who inspired me by telling me to keep writing. For the rest of my family, thank you for your support in all that I do.

Table of Contents

Memories Interrupted
    Chapter One   1

A Bat?
    Chapter Two   19

A Wise Friend
    Chapter Three   32

A Strange Squabble Indeed
    Chapter Four   45

Clean, but how?
    Chapter Five   57

New Information
    Chapter Six   64

Remarkable Bird
    Chapter Seven   85

A Decent Meal
    Chapter Eight: 97

Dragons?
    Chapter Nine   107

The New World
    Chapter Ten   119

Totally Amazing
    Chapter Eleven   131

A Crocowolf
    Chapter Twelve   162

The Invasion
    Chapter Thirteen   177

The Blazing Fire
    Chapter Fourteen   201

A Midnight Ride
    Chapter Fifteen   210

A Great Christmas.
    Chapter Sixteen   221

The Talk with the Count
    Chapter Seventeen   227

A Kid with a Grudge
    Chapter Eighteen   252

The Scene in the Viewer
    Chapter Nineteen   265

Departure
    Chapter Twenty   274

Memories Interrupted

CHAPTER ONE

Max Morgan was a rather pale boy, and far too scrawny— this, of course, was absolutely not his fault. He would have been fairly pleased to gain a pound or two, particularly to keep his backside from aching while sitting on a hard chair in one of many boring classes. His light brown hair was straight as straw and kept short; his deep ivy- green eyes had a sprinkling of coffee -colored specks in them. Unfortunately he was a tad clumsy and a bit awkward. At twelve years of age that's to be expected. What was not to be expected was that he was, in fact, an orphan. Lastly, he hadn't a clue that somewhere far away two curious beings watched him intently.

At this very moment, Max was on a quest of sneaking down to the class room in order to deposit his overdue English assignment into the papers due basket. He had hoped no one would notice him out of his room this late in the evening. Regrettably that was not the case, as a black erasure full of chalk dust, was hurled through the air and met the side of Max's head with a thump. Lenny, who had also been turning in a past due paper, had seized the opportunity to whiten the unwary Max with a thick layer of chalk.

It was half past nine, and the quiet calm had suddenly been replaced by grunts and crashes as the two ill tempered boys began thrashing one another. Max had been unable to remain level headed after the stinging slap from the erasure and the burning dryness in his eye caused from the chalk powder. And because of Max's failure to turn the other cheek— so to speak, Lenny's closed fist in a well aimed wallop encompassed Max's nose and mouth creating a splattering of blood across Max's long lashed eyelids. He stood in the English room swaying from side to side, his breathing came in ragged gulps; blood poured from the cut inside his lip while his tongue detected a loose front tooth. The blood trickling down his throat was making him queasy. Another blow landed at the corner of his left eye sending him reeling backwards, falling like a brick to the floor.

While Max lay splayed across the floor Lenny stepped up to him and extended his leg for one final kick. Taking Lenny by surprise Max's foot had connected squarely to the vulnerable zone between Lenny's legs. He was sent rocketing across the room crashing to the floor in pain. Lenny lay at the base of the book case while Max scrambled to his feet and stood motionless in an effort to catch his breath, and to recover some sense of balance. His anger squeezed the air from his lungs.

Surprising both of them, the books on the shelves began to pummel Lenny and now he lay buried in a very large pile. Max stared in amazement while Lenny clambered out from under the enormous mound of paper, cardboard, and print.

Seconds later the two boys stood there shouting insults to each other when Mr. Crater and Mrs. Rosenblam appeared, grabbing each of the students by the collars while assessing the disarray. "My room! Look what you two have done! What is the reason for this outrageous behavior?" Mrs. Rosenblam shouted.

"Who cares about the 'reason,' the floor in my office needs to be washed," Mr. Crater roared, pulling the boys to the back of the building where his grubby office smelling of cigarette smoke and other hard to identify odors hung in the air.

The boys' disheveled, swollen appearance combined with the dried blood seemed almost tidy compared to the filthy floor. Layers of dirt, grease, and the deep shoe indentations gave them the realization this would be no ordinary job. The adults left to retrieve scrub brushes and a bucket containing soap and water.

"If you hadn't been such a sissy this never would have happened, it's entirely your fault," Lenny spat.

"What? Defending myself from the eraser you threw at me? No, it was definitely your fault." Max glared past his half closed eyelid.

"It was just an eraser; you didn't have to punch me in the ear. Now look what we're forced to do all night." Lenny kicked a large pile of cigarette butts across the floor.

"Serves you both right!" Mr. Crater said slamming down the bucket with a slosh, while Mrs. Rosenblam threw them each a scrub brush. "Have a nice evening." She sneered, "you will pick up the books in my room when this floor is finished, then you may go to your room." She emphasized the word finished with a hiss.

While the boys took out their frustration on the filthy floor, icy winds and cold December sleet pounded outside the window of the old, towering building at 64 Crudder Street.

Deep into the night with aching arms and knees, the boys, at last, could actually see what appeared to be the floor boards. Their anger dissipated as the night wore on. Max couldn't think of anyone he hated more than Lenny. Regardless of that deep-seated hatred he was glad to have had the help for a short time—of course Lenny had long since left telling Max he could finish the rest since it had been 'his fault.' Early into the morning hours Max tossed the worn, dirty brush back into the bucket with a splat and stood to leave the office and return to his room.

As he stretched his aching back his gaze met the sinister black eyes of a man in a painting standing next to a jagged rocky ledge. Most of the painting was Dark and hard to decipher. Max had to strain his tired eyes to take in the full haughtiness of the Man who was impeccably dressed in black, his smooth combed hair shining and slick in a V shape that appeared etched on his forehead. The Woman standing next to the man was unkempt and grimy as were the two small children, their gaunt bodies made Max look plump. Max could instinctually tell that the man was cruel and feared by the others. He stepped up to the painting for a closer look— the fearful look on the woman and children's faces made Max frown while the man's eyes seemed to bore into his very core.

Max reached up and ran his hand across the rough -painted surface, wondering who these people were. Unexpectedly a burning snap to his fingers made him recoil; his hand had been zapped with what he assumed was static electricity. With a shudder he backed away from the eerie sight and left the office, his aching body hobbled down the corridor. Hearing the voices of Mrs. Rosenblam and Mr. Crater, he paused outside the door to the English room. Peering in, he was relieved to see the books had already been neatly placed on the shelves by someone else—he wondered who since Mrs. Rosenblam had told them they were to do that before they went to their room and Max was positive that neither they nor Lenny would have picked them up. Max stood just outside the door and listened.

"I fired her. She said she was appalled by the conditions of this place and by the food and the punishments we give out." Mr. Crater said

"She was hardly here a day, now what will we do about history lessons? Don't you dare look at me! I will not teach that subject again; one class with these idiots is enough," Mrs. Rosenblam spat. Her voice high pitched and tinged with anger.

"Well then," Mr. Crater snarled, "they don't need history, the brats don't pay any attention anyway, no one cares about them. Since we don't answer to anyone and I run this place, we won't worry about history."

"Suppose she tells someone?" asked Mrs. Rosenblam.

"Suppose she does. No one knows we exist; there are only a handful of us that show up here day after day. Nothing new except the occasional little orphan who wanders in— highlight of my day," he drawled the last bit sarcastically.

Max was now positive that he would get no reprieve from this place; there would be no one to put a stop to the deplorable conditions. He was stuck, they all were. He made his way past the office and to his dorm room.

The confines of the shabby room were littered with books, papers, and clothes of the inhabitant's. Spiders, mice, and cockroaches scurried around the room paying no attention to the sleeping students whose only protection from the icy air was thin, grimy blankets used by all of the many unfortunates who had entered these walls. Slow steady breaths emitted a white mist with each exhalation. The tiny ten-by-ten dormitory room smelled like a locker room.

Max sat on the edge of his cot removing his shoes and clothes, slipping on his only pair of pajamas he laid down. He struggled to find a comfortable position; his body ached in every possible location. With a deep sigh, his mind played over the last three years in the orphanage. His days were filled with the ritual of being teased and taunted by the others. He was cautious about where he sat since the other kids, mostly Lenny, stuck glue, gum, tacks, and the occasional dead rodent or insect on his seat. At times he would stick up for himself, which would lead to him having to stay after class to clean the floors and pick up the garbage. A few incidents came to mind: one in which Lenny had put a big black stink beetle down the back of Max's shirt and smashed it; wet gooey guts and the horrible odor followed him for days. Although Lenny was at fault, Max was the one to stand at the blackboard with his nose in a circle for the rest of the day – five hours in all.

He drew himself into a ball on the lumpy cot, covering his head with the bag of torn paper that acted as his pillow, while he tried to remember a happier time.

It had regrettably been three years since he'd lived with Gramps on the farm. With his eyes closed he visualized the old farm house covered with peeling white paint, the red barn with its dry sun scorched surface and patched roof. Inside the barn beneath the loft, mounds of hay lay in forgotten heaps. Under the barns rafters black bats of many sizes hung out unconcernedly until evening fell when they would dive through the dark emitting high- pitched squeals.

"Ouch!" Max sat up, rubbed his head, and looked around. A heavy brown shoe lay on his chest, thrown by someone across the room. Seizing hold of the shoe, he sat up noticing a faint light intruded through the small, dirty window proving he must've fallen asleep after all. Shattering his peaceful memories was the growling repulsive voice of Lenny Brummel. "Hey, creep, you're daydreaming again. It's time to get ready for class; not that any one wants you around, but I'm sure they'll need someone to pickup garbage," Lenny snarled dismissively. Glowering at Max, Lenny jerked his shoe from Max's hand before stomping out the door. Max ran his hand over his still- swollen and, bruised face. To Max's disappointment Lenny had not looked nearly as bloodied and bruised as he had hoped.

Max thought about Lenny. He was mean, loud and obnoxious and seemed perfectly content to be so. He and his buddies, Rubin Tank and Gorfus Silva all slept in the same room, taking great pleasure in irritating Max day and night.

Five students shared each tiny room and the orphanage kept a total of twenty kids, most of whom enjoyed a laugh each time Max was the object of ridicule.

Max stepped out onto the cold, wooden floor dodging the scurrying insects. Groggily he walked over to the small crate that held his belongings. He had only three outfits and since his dirty clothes had not yet been returned from the laundry he was down to only one. Everything he owned, with the exception of one small box of possessions, were hand-me-downs from those who already left the school. Grabbing the same outfit he had worn for nearly four days (this one in particular must have belonged to a third grader because it fit like a shrunken sweater) he returned to his cot, sat down on the edge to dress; finally, pulling on his worn socks and scuffed leather shoes. As he grabbed a tattered old coat from the crate, he looked fondly at the dark box sitting at the bottom; it was filled with the items given to him by his Gramps for Max's ninth birthday. Max remembered it as though it were yesterday. September twentieth. He could almost feel the cool air and the bright afternoon sun against his skin. He took a deep breath wishing he could smell the fresh air of that day. He recalled the trees covered with brilliant orange, red, and yellow leaves.

Gramps told Max he had an unusual birthday gift for him and he led Max to the barn where they climbed the steps to the loft. The sweet smell of hay and the decaying scent of old leather from the saddles and bridles wafted through the air. A mound of yellowing straw stood stacked in the corner. At the opposite end, old, dry, cracked leather bridles lay strewn about. One discarded saddle lay in a heap on the floor; the once supple leather now dried and wrinkled. The sheep skin underside lay in fluffy mounds mixed with hay and bits of chewed debris acting as a warm nest for the mice who claimed the barn as their home.

A cool breeze fluttered through the door in the loft, chilling their skin. As they topped the steps, Max could hardly contain his excitement. He sat down on the floor beneath the huge door frame, dangling his legs out twenty feet above the ground. Gramps walked over to the giant trunk that had always been a curious item with its massive rusted lock looking most impenetrable. Gramps was now rummaging through the belly of the trunk, pulling out items and setting them aside.

Max felt a bit apprehensive while waiting, his uncertainty evident on his face. Finally, Gramps pulled out a worn wooden box, he grinned broadly while he carefully placed the other items back in the trunk. After he snapped the lock shut, he joined Max on the floor then carefully opened the lid, and placed several gadgets in Max's hands.

The first was an odd black stone the size of a walnut with a smooth surface on one side and sharp points on the other. Max held the stone and felt the different textures as he rolled it in his hands. Next was a peculiar pocket knife—solid and aged. The blades of this knife were razor sharp. Setting sunlight reflected off a narrow strip of copper a touch bigger then a stick of gum; Max could see his reflection in it and the puzzled look on his face. He wasn't sure exactly how to react as more items were presented to him. Gramps pulled out a silver skeleton key which looked new —it had maybe never opened a lock.

A bizarre kind of map was spread on the floor for Max to assess, raised mounds lifted several inches high while deep crevices encircled several gray patches. As Max ran his fingers over the map, he noticed chillingly that the blue areas of the map actually dampened his fingertips. Failing to note the stunned look fixed on Max's face, his Gramps presented him with two worn, brown- leather gloves that looked as though they'd been passed down through generations. As he slipped them on, they wrapped themselves around his hands for a perfect fit; an electrical sensation had zapped at his fingers. He pulled them off quickly replacing them in the box.

Gramps chuckled as though he knew what had caused the sensation, he skirted the issue saying, "Max, these are special items, the time will come when you'll know what to do with them. For now, keep them in the box. Only bring them out when the time is right."

Max was perplexed. "Uh- sir how will I know the time is right?"

"You'll know because the secret these items carry will be revealed to you when you are old enough to understand." Gramps said as he gave Max a penetrating look to underscore the importance of the information he was conveying. Max of course, didn't understand much of the conversation or the significance of the items; he trusted

Gramps to be honest with him, yet inwardly he thought Gramps was probably losing it.

The sun disappeared behind the distant mountains. Visible in the sky was the red orange smattering of color on the horizon, the shadows nearly fading; a faint cry of the killdeer reminded them that darkness would soon erase any trace of light.

As they stood to leave, Gramps ruffled his hair, "Max, everything that I told you will make perfect sense one day when you're ready. It did for me when I was your age and all those before us. As for me losing it— I am not." Max's shocked expression and the uneasy shuffle of his feet brought a twinkle to the older man's blue eyes. With that, they strolled back to the house. Max was particularly uncomfortable with the last statement Gramps made, almost as though he had read Max's thoughts. It was eerie.

A loud crash outside the small room snapped Max back to the present. He was both saddened and comforted by his memories. He carefully replaced the box back in his crate and headed down stairs to join the breakfast line. His daydreaming cost him some time and he was almost late; he decided to jog the rest of the way to the cafeteria. As he approached, Lenny stuck his foot out, sending Max sailing into the middle of the floor. Smacking his face on the dirty wood, his left nostril discharged a slow trickle of blood; he reached up with his sleeve and wiped it away. Lying on his belly in front of everyone, Max groaned, his face red with anger and embarrassment. He wiped his nose again and looked up, trying not to notice the other kids laughing and pointing his direction. From out of nowhere Rubin stepped over Max's sore, motionless body. "You really should be more careful, you clumsy nerd. While you're down there want a scrub brush?" Rubin chuckled, as he nearly stepped on Max's hand.

"Yeah, you should be more careful," Gorfus shouted as he too marched over the top of Max. Another round of laughs and snickers echoed through the cafeteria as Max struggled to regain his composure.

Max smothered the urge to walk over and kick all three of them in the teeth, but instead he clamored to his feet; rubbed his bruised palms against his side, and wiped at the now dry blood under his nose. He wouldn't give any of them the satisfaction by showing his pain. Max collected his meager meal and carried his tray to the table; he sat down next to Sam Springfield and Tracie Miller.

Tracie smiled at him, patting his shoulder affectionately. Her brown eyes warmly welcomed him, taking in the blood stained shirt, swollen lip, black eye and now the bloodied nose. "Oh", she faltered "what happened to your face? That couldn't have all happened just now!"

Max shook his head, "Lenny and I had a petty disagreement last night, after which we ended up cleaning Crater's floor." He added furiously, "it wasn't a bit fun."

"You look terrible," Sam mumbled sympathetically through a mouthful of dry toast as he peered closer.

"Yeah, thanks, I don't feel much better then I look." Max recounted the evening's incidence to his friends.

Tracie pointed to Max's nose. "You have just a speck of blood there under your nose."

"Thanks." Max murmured glumly and wiped it away with his shirt sleeve.

Tracie changed the subject in an attempt to lighten the mood; she stirred the sticky looking mush in her bowl, "Look at this; this is incredible. The cooks have certainly outdone themselves with this slop." Tracie continued contemptuously. "It would seem to me that they would feed us better so that we could concentrate on something other then our growling stomachs. You know, a good use for this would be to stick those three oafs to the wall," she pointed her spoon full of mush towards Lenny and his friends who were now throwing food and goofing around.

"Hey, yeah now that's a good use for this." Sam said, picking up a spoonful and letting the slimy, gray-green, hot cereal slop off his spoon. They got a good laugh, even Max was becoming more contented by the minute, regardless of his swollen, bloody face, skinned hands and bruised ego. Max ate his dry toast and drank the warm water which tasted as he imagined pond water would taste.

There was no way he could stomach the slop. He grimaced and pushed the bowl away.

As they were eating, the snotty Miss Arabeth Portly limped into the room, her usually perfect makeup was smudged and her hair was rumpled. They watched as she sat down at the table with Lenny.

"I just don't get it." Tracie said. "Lenny stomps on her foot and breaks her toe, she still hangs out with him and to top it off she looks at him as though he were a king or something." Tracie rolled her eyes.

"They deserve each other though, don't you think?" Max asked pretending to flip back his hair, imitating Arabeth.

"Yeah, actually they're a lot alike." Sam said, also pretended to flip his hair back as they laughed. Tracie had to admit she would love to have the golden mane of hair that Arabeth had, however she doubted it would look as good on her. Arabeth was, after all, a very nice looking girl— of course, it did take a lot of effort, she would primp for hours before class and late into the night after class.

Tracie brought up the subject of the upcoming Christmas party when the school would serve one meal of edible food and give the kids five days off for vacation, which was at least something. No one had family, at least none who wanted them around, so they had to make their own fun. Max was having trouble concentrating on his friends' conversation. He was distracted by the view across the room at the table where Lenny sat visiting with Mrs. Rosenblam.

Max suddenly sat bolt upright, bitterly saying. "We can't let Lenny, Rubin and Gorfus steal the gifts and food or do anything else to ruin the party. All the things that they find entertaining are bad for the rest of us."

Tracie groaned miserably in agreement. "Yeah, I'm just sorry they usually find a way to destroy anything nice."

"They're the ones who should be sorry! They ruin everything year after year and it gets worse as they get more creative," Max said scornfully.

"We should do something rotten to them this year," Sam said. "After what they did last year, they don't deserve to have Christmas."

"Especially what they did to you Max." Tracie frowned with empathy in her eyes.

Max nodded. The memories of the previous year came flooding back to Max, the evil trio had put cockroaches in the pumpkin pie and a dead rat on the turkey platter. Then they threw the turkey down the laundry chute where no one could find the bird until it started to smell. Everyone was forced to eat liver for dinner, as usual.

Each year the students received one gift from the staff, usually a pencil, a crayon, or a notebook. Max, Tracie, and Sam's gifts were missing from the gift table, so they got nothing. The smirk on Lenny's face told them he had something to do with the gifts' disappearance.

The worst thing was when a note, addressed to Max was received by Mr. Crater, the principle. The note said his grandfather would be there to pick him up on Christmas Eve and that Max should watch for him. Max was very excited to be going home, he had dreamed of this moment for years. He sat on his crate with his eyes peering out the window at the cold darkness. He patiently waited for automobile lights to approach the building from the rarely traveled road. He mulled over in his head what he would say to his Gramps. He visualized his gramps sitting behind the wheel of his old dark green and rust colored ford tuck.

Sometime late into the night he had fallen asleep; his wet face smashed against the glass snoring loudly. Daylight crept in when Max was awakened by a loud chorus of laughter. His still blurry eyes opened to find Lenny, Rubin and Gorfus laughing hysterically while holding their bellies. Lenny shouted between bursts of laughter. "Looks like old gramps don't want you after all." They left the room still laughing while Max felt dejected and angry. It was a joke and a very cruel one at that. Max knew Lenny was the one who set it up, no one else knew about the letter except Tracie, Sam and, of course, Mr. Crater who had grunted loudly since he had been inconvenienced by having to give the letter to Max.

This year Max thought things would be different he would ignore any letters or any other peculiar gags those creeps came up with. Max put his elbows on the table, resting his chin in his hands as he watched the exchange taking place across the room. Lenny and Mrs. Rosenblam were still deep in animated chitchat. The conversation reminded Max of a trained dog eager to fetch its master's stick. There was no doubt in his mind they were up to no good. Lenny's square head bobbled up and down as though it were attached with a spring. Max watched, waiting for Lenny to start wagging his tail and panting. Max wished he was sitting close enough to hear what they were conspiring. He was positive that if it were a plot against him, he would find out all too soon.

A Bat?

CHAPTER TWO

The clanging bell in the hallway warned everyone it was time for first period classes. Max's day began with the grouchiest teacher of all—Mrs. Rosenblam. Her face reminded him of a bearded lizard with her pointy nose and the long flap of skin that hung down under her chin; her scowl seemed written with durable ink. Her coal-black hair was pulled tightly into a bun and lay perched atop her scrawny head; she was tall, slender, and pale. Her cold mannerisms left most students feeling frostbit after an encounter with her. Lenny was the exception. He strived hard to become teacher's pet, succeeding nicely with his phony personality and his wide, fake toothy grin; which he never hesitated to flash in order to get his way. Their scheming against Max, gave him the misfortune of being the butt of their jokes. The laughs she received made her face twist in an ugly lopsided smirk whenever she belittled him in front of everyone.

The subject she taught was English. As always, Max was content to sit in the back of the room and go unnoticed. However, Mrs. R liked to embarrass him by asking him to stand and answer questions. Max kept up with the assignments and could usually answer her questions, but today his mind began drifting near the end of her class. His wandering mind was jolted back by Mrs. R shouting "Mr. Morgan, are you sleeping on my time? Up too late? Or could it be that you think it's too boring to sit and listen? Maybe you have to be kept busy doing something other then sitting?"

"Yes! I mean no," Max stammered. How could he answer that! He was caught red-handed, and whatever punishment she meted out would more than likely take him all night to finish. He had been down that road before with her; remembering back how he spent five hours scrubbing her floor with a torn up old sponge because he accidentally tripped over Lenny's fat foot and bumped into her, causing her to spill her coffee all over the front of her. She of course was several shades of angry.

"Well, then, Mr. Morgan, maybe you'd pay more attention if you put a little more effort into your work. After school, you will return to your seat in this room. You will copy word-for-word the first six chapters of this English book." She held up the enormous book. That meant he'd still be writing the next morning when class started. Max slumped down in his seat. He felt that familiar diminished feeling he experienced when Mrs. Rosenblam put him down in front of the class. The other kids were gawking and snickering at him. A deep scarlet flush warmed his face. Tracie and Sam shook their heads, looking as though they'd like to banish Mrs. R from the planet for her cruelness.

The rest of the morning passed without incident. Sam, Tracie, and Max sat together at lunch trying to eat their liver sandwiches and cabbage soup. "Same lunch as yesterday only worse I didn't think it possible for this food to get older and dryer," Sam moaned. He rapped on the table with his sandwich— the dry, molding bread sounded like a block of wood.

"Yeah, I wish just once we were served maybe a hamburger or pepperoni pizza." Max's mouth began to water, yet stopped straightaway as he peered forlornly down at the brown liver nestled between the hunks of greenish bread. Max pushed it away and glanced at Tracie who had her head in the English book. "I didn't know you liked that awful English class well enough to study at lunch!"

She slammed the book shut. "I definitely do not! I was looking to see how bad you're night's going to be. Each of these chapters has almost twenty pages in it," She said aghast.

"Yeah, don't remind me. I'm thinking I'll be busy," Max said with a hint of dread.

"Maybe we can sneak down and help you copy them," Tracie whispered.

"What, and take a chance on getting old lizard face mad at you? No, I'll be okay. At least I won't have to be closed up in the dorm with

Lenny, Rubin, and Gorfus tonight." Max made a sour face. "Sorry, Sam, but you'll be stuck with them all alone."

Sam grinned and hit his open hand with his fist, "No witnesses." They snickered.

Lunch ended with the clanging of the bell; trudging out into the hall and to the next class was an effort. Slate gray sky brought depressing yawns in sequence beginning with Max, then Sam and finally Tracie. Max heaved a big sigh, "Next class I suppose."

An uneventful, even uninteresting afternoon ebbed on; Max however began to dread the end of the school day worse than the long boring lectures and the insurmountable homework that was building up.

Finally after a snail's pace there it was the last bell of the day. All the students exited the school rooms heading for the dorms in order to stash their books and papers and race to the cafeteria for their tidbit of food. With his dinner only partially eaten Max bid Tracie and Sam good-night, telling Sam he'd see him before midnight—maybe.

"Well, good luck then." Sam smiled and smacked him on the back as Max sauntered down the hallway to the English room.

The windows looked out over the desolate grounds with its harsh wire fence; and the dark, ominous pond. The water in the pond was dark and thick, having no resemblance whatsoever to what water ought to be. Surrounding the pond dead decaying undergrowth hid piles of rubbish. The area around there never bloomed, nor turned green; come to think of it, not much around there did bloom or turn green. It was always dank and dreary.

Max stood at the window as the dark of the night crept up. He thought he could see shadows lurking behind the mounds of rubbish; a broken tree limb appeared to move closer to the window. The eerie view brought distorted images to his mind. A loud thump broke the silence as a tree limb smacked against the window causing Max to duck. A quiver quickened his pulse as he wasted little time leaving the window. After all, he was alone in the cold spooky room; alone in the whole building it seemed, not even the old clock on the wall made a sound. Taking his seat he began copying sentences from the English book.

Hours slowly slipped away, he'd reached the third chapter, but still Mrs. Rosenblam hadn't arrived. That was strange; any other time she'd be there to gloat over him, looking down her long nose while glaring her bloodshot eyes at him. She seemed to really enjoy that part of her job. She reveled in the chance to make rude comments about his work, or his hair, his grubby clothes or some other obvious shortcoming. He wondered how she could be missing this. What could be more important?

He continued the tedious assignment as his hand cramped. It was nearly ten and all was quiet. While he was finishing up the third chapter he was startled by a loud slam and then another. Max stood and went to the door. As he peered around the corner, Mr. Crater, the principal, stepped up to him from the other side and growled, "What are you doing down here at this hour?" Bits of smelly spit splattered out of his mouth landing on Max's face. Automatically he tilted his head to the side and quickly wiped it away on his shoulder. Staring down at his tattered shoes Max choked out a noise somewhat like a hesitant bullfrog then anxiously replied. "I was copying chapters for Mrs. Rosenblam."

"I am not surprised as I'm sure you were a complete pain in the neck today, huh Morgan? I would have thought after last night's deed that tonight you may want to behave, but trouble just follows you around everywhere you go. Almost like the foul stench that clings to you." Mr. Crater took a deep whistling breath through his nose folding even more wrinkles into his wrinkling face. He advanced on Max, bitterness etched on his face. Mr. Crater's greasy hair matched the one long eyebrow hovering over both eyes. Nearly seven feet tall, he towered above Max. His teeth were yellow from smoking, his breath smelled of rotting liver, reminding Max of what they served in the cafeteria. Everyone knew this man did not like kids.

"No. I was just day dreaming a little, that's all." Max hedged.

"Well, I suppose you were wishing you were somewhere else, huh Morgan? But I have you until you turn eighteen, so get used to it and stop wishing otherwise, that is, of course, unless you're Gramps sends another letter of intent to take you away from here this Christmas and actually shows up." His ugly head flew back and he laughed a hideous, barking sound that echoed through the corridor. One final grunt and he lumbered off down the hall, leaving Max shaken and extremely livid.

"You have me until I'm eighteen only because I have no choice," Max grumbled stubbornly. "And that smell was your own breath." The reference to his Gramps made Max wonder if Mr. Crater could have had something to do with the fraudulent letter nearly a year ago. Max returned to his desk and began finishing up the chapters.

Several hours later, a scuffling noise awakened him. He'd fallen asleep with his head pressed against the book and was now shivering with cold. He looked around, trying to remember what he was doing there, only to realize the window stood wide open. The bone chilling wind came crashing in uninvited. Max rushed over to close it. The room was calm and quiet, so who had opened the window? Max sat back down and picked up his pen, intending to finish his assignment.

The hair on the back of his neck stood up and the room spun as he looked at the page in front of him. His work was completed. He could remember finishing the third chapter, but not the fourth, fifth, and sixth. What was going on? This was definitely his handwriting. But how could it be? Glancing at the clock, he saw it was nearly three in the morning.

He was far too tired to ponder it further. Closing the book, he left the room and wandered up the long hallway, he listened to boards in the floor groan. All the lights were out except the occasional night light along the base of the wall. He didn't need a light—he knew his way by memory. He'd been up and down these halls a million times.

The lower level of the building contained classrooms, a crude library, the offices, and the cafeteria. The second level held meeting rooms, the nurse's room, which by the way contained no nurse. Also on the second floor were the restrooms, and the big room where the students had activities on their short breaks; they were seldom allowed outside. The third floor housed the few staff members who stayed on the grounds and also contained a series of locked rooms which to Max's knowledge none of the students had ever seen. Students were housed on the fourth floor, in the attic—five bedrooms and two shower rooms. It also housed the fourth floor room-keeper Mrs. Twill; a short, grouchy woman with long, snarled gray hair, missing front teeth, and a nose covering the better part of her face which could explain why she seemed able to smell a student who was not where they were supposed to be. Her job was to clean up and keep an eye on students in the evenings.

A horrible feeling shattered Max's leisurely walk, when swiftly something black whooshed past his head. Picking up the pace he rounded the corner, cut through the cafeteria, and hurried to the winding staircase. His hand reached for the gnarled wood hand rail, with white knuckles protruding an uneasy panic rose in his throat. Whatever was fluttering around made him uncomfortable.

He took the steps two at a time up the winding stairs past the first three floors. As he walked through the hall to the next staircase he was startled to see a fat, hairy mouse sitting on the handrail, watching him.

Max had never seen such a huge mouse. Looking closer he realized it was actually a bat, the papery wings now apparent in the faint light. He peered closer, while two large emerald green eyes peered back. Max noted that it was actually a green-eyed bat; he moved first left, then right as the animal kept track of him with its jewel like eyes. His heart thumped and a chill raced up his spine into his hair, he had the distinct feeling that his hair was standing on end. He rubbed the top of his head in an effort to ease the prickling feeling.

The bat's eyes were speaking to him. Entering Max's psyche was the simple declaration. "Hang in there and things will get better."

Max backed against the banister, his legs felt as though they were not receiving the run message that his brain was sending them. He stood motionless while the words entered his head as though a loud speaker had been placed next to his ears. "I need you to believe things will get better." The words were clear as was their meaning. But due to Max's alarm he could not make them register. All he wanted to do was to run and hide, preferably sooner than later. At the top of the staircase, he saw a familiar black bird watching him, it tipped its head curiously to one side and then to the other. It dawned on Max that he had seen this bird on several occasions. At least he thought it was the same bird. His first day at the orphanage it had observed him for several hours. Max vigorously rubbed his eyes, causing them to burn; his gaze darted to the bat then to the bird. He thought for a moment that he must still be in the English room sleeping and all of this was a bizarre dream. Max shook his head; he rubbed his eyes again to clear his vision, he mumbled over several times, "I'm just tired I need to get some rest." His mutterings and a few deep breaths calmed him, making him feel better.

Suddenly, he heard the words vibrate in his head, "Max, my boy, you're fine. Just stay safe and stop giving these poor excuses for teachers a reason to be meaner then usual. See you soon."

Max shut his eyes tightly, tongue-tied; he thought to himself there is no bat or bird it's my mind playing tricks on me. He must be going crazy—or maybe he just needed sleep. When he looked again, the bat and the bird had disappeared. Now he knew he was crazy; he'd just had a telepathic conversation with a bat. Letting out a long sigh Max looked around to make sure he was truly alone then he sprinted up the steps with the feeling that something was chasing him.

Max entered the smelly room, collapsing on his cot he curled up and covered his head with the blanket. Sleep didn't come rapidly, despite the fact that he was exhausted. The idea of flying bats talking to him invaded his sleep and made the next few hours restless. Finally he entered a deep sleep twenty minutes before his roommates began rousing for the morning routine. He awoke as daylight began to show traces of a dreary wet day.

He pulled himself from his cot, memories of the night before flooded back. Everything seemed so real; the window opening, his school work getting done without any memory of doing it, the bird and the bat talking to him. What a night! He was certainly not going to daydream in Mrs. R's class today. He doubted he could survive another night like that.

He tied his shoe laces, asking himself, if it really all happened or was it the result of his imagination? It sure felt real.

At breakfast Max told Tracie and Sam about his strange experience. They looked at one another frowning, obviously doubting his tale. Tracie broke the awkward silence by giggling and saying, "You almost had us believing you were serious, Max."

"I am serious," Max mumbled, lowering his head and frowning. "I hoped when I told you about it I could laugh it off, but now I wonder if I'm going crazy. Or maybe someone's playing a joke on me."

Sam laughed. "That must be it! Lenny, Gorfus, and Rubin are probably getting a good laugh about now."

"I thought about that," Max said. "But why would they help me finish my English assignment? And besides, it was my own handwriting."

Sam shrugged. "Yeah that is way out of character —" stopping mid -sentence Sam looked as though he were not sure if Max knew what he had just told them— "really, it was your own handwriting?"

"Maybe you wrote the last few chapters in your sleep. People are capable of doing strange things when they are asleep; I once heard of a girl who did all of her laundry while she slept, she had no idea she had done it. So you see it really is possible." Tracie affirmed.

Max ignored Tracie, his mind was occupied. "Sure." He tried to smile. "There has to be a logical explanation."

Their morning meal was hurled into the trash while their stomachs gave off a persistent rumble; they wandered off to the first class of the day. Mrs. Rosenblam stood at the head of the class smirking when they entered the room. She patiently waited until all the students had taken their seats before she began. "Mr. Morgan did you have a nice evening? I see you managed to get these pages copied." She held the papers aloft for a moment, and then tossed them all into the trash can. The other students laughed. Max bristled, it wasn't as if he were surprised by her lack of regard for his hard work, he just really wanted to throw something at her.

Max clenched his fists, but kept his thoughts to himself. He didn't dare give her another excuse to keep him after school. Tracie looked as though she too had some thoughts she'd like to express, but no one said a word. The moment passed and Mrs. Rosenblam looked disappointed that Max had kept his mouth shut. Max felt a kind of rush at having bested the old hag.

The remainder of English passed quietly—no more problems. The reptilian woman did however seem very disappointed when the students got up to leave and she still could not find a reason to keep him after school. Max had to smile at her obvious annoyance. The next three classes moved quickly; Max managed to stay out of trouble, though he had difficulty keeping his eyes open.

Afternoon crept up, the clouds outside grew darker while the chill in the building deepened. Max would have been content to just gaze out over the ugly grounds until he fell asleep, but he had to keep up with the subjects or he'd end up staying after class and doing rotten jobs for the other teachers. He was determined to make it through the rest of the day.

A Wise Friend

CHAPTER THREE

Math class finally arrived—the last period of the day. Max was afraid he might not be able to stay awake, so he asked Tracie and Sam to kick him if he dozed off. He could barely concentrate on the long division problems because his thoughts kept returning to the night before; he played every possible scenario he could through his mind, but he still couldn't explain what had happened.

"Hey!" A paper airplane came out of nowhere and hit him squarely between the eyes. Looking around, he saw no one had even noticed. Max opened it and read:

"Don't worry so much, you are certainly not losing your mind. And Max, please smile."

Max stared at the paper and looked around the room to see if anyone was watching and could give him a clue where the note had come from. He held the note in his hand and attempted to slide the note to Sam who sat concentrating on the lesson, oblivious to what had just happened.

"Hey Sam," Max whispered.

Suddenly, Mr. Brittle, the math teacher, a short, round-faced, balding man who resembled a mushroom walked up, snatched the paper away, and told Max,

"We do not pass notes in this or any other class, Mr. Morgan." His short stubby fingers held the paper up to his tiny watery eyes. In an attempt to read it, he turned it over and then over again. Looking baffled, he handed it back to Max and stammered, "Keep your paper to yourself," Mr. Brittle wheezed. He was always short of breath, and his chest rose rapidly with each gulp of air. He had nearly no neck so it looked as though his head was merely resting on his broad shoulders and it appeared to rock forward as he filled his lungs. Even without a neck, or the ability to turn his head without turning his whole body, he was able to catch nearly everything going on in his class. He would load them up with huge assignments at the first of class. Then he would plod around the class room standing behind each of the students puffing like a freight train. He was not mean, he was just annoying,

Max was puzzled. The writing on the paper had vanished. He looked around the room, feeling self- conscious, but no one else paid any attention to him. Had there been words on that paper? Oh, boy! He needed some rest. Mr. Brittle waddled to the front of the class;

his ample back end filled and exceeded the stool he plopped onto. At that very moment the bell clanged and Mr. Brittle had to shout out, above the shuffling papers and sliding of chairs in his whining voice, "alright students settle down and remember you need to finish all of chapter nine, ten, and eleven by the end of the week. That only gives you three days, so work hard."

Max left his desk; wearing a dazed look, he walked out of the math room talking to himself. "The writing was there! Or was it?" He turned the paper over, held it up to the hall lights, and turned it over again.

Tracie and Sam walked up beside him. "What's up, Max?" Sam asked.

Max held up the creased sheet of paper. "It was as clear as could be. It read. *Don't worry so much, you are most certainly not losing your mind. And Max, please smile.* But the writing vanished when Mr. Brittle grabbed it."

"What do you mean—vanished?" Tracie frowned.

"Vanished, Gone, as in it wasn't on the paper when Mr. Brittle looked at it, or when he handed it back to me." Max unfolded the paper, shoving it at them. "See, nothing" he said.

"Max, come on, this is unreal. Are you sure it was there in the first place?" Sam asked.

"No, I'm not sure of anything, right now." Max shot off down the hall leaving his friends confused and alarmed.

"Well," Tracie said, "He's been under a lot of stress. Maybe a good night's sleep will help."

"Or maybe it's genetic, Tracie. You know what they say about his Grandpa going crazy and sending him away. Max might be going crazy." Tracie shook her head, "I doubt it, he's just tired." She paused, "I really don't think he has suddenly lost his mind; but maybe that crack on the head from Lenny has caused him to— oh, never mind." They ambled up the steps in preoccupied silence. Tracie waved goodnight. "I've got a mountain of reading to catch up on, I think I'll tuck in and do just that, I certainly have no appetite so I think I'll skip dinner. Goodnight."

"Night Tracie." Sam waved and headed off to his room.

Max had hurried to his room and flopped onto the cot, hoping to grab an hour's sleep before the other boys returned. Once again, sleep didn't come. Over and over in his mind, he ran through the unsettling events of the afternoon and the day before.

Could it be that he himself was in fact losing his mind as rumor had it his gramps had. He thought about the day three years earlier, in September, a week after his birthday. The night had been quiet and cool; the last faint sounds of a few diehard crickets and frogs filled the air as well as the mournful cry of a coyote in the distance. He and Gramps sat outside on the front porch, passing the time together; it had been a great day.

They saw lights on the gravel road, and then heard the sound of engines. A few minutes later, three cars pulled up to the porch. A trio of grim-looking police officers walked up the steps and faced them. Seth Peters, the town sheriff, approached Gramps. To Max's surprise, Gramps looked as though he'd been expecting them.

"Evening Ben —Max," the sheriff said. "Guess you know why we're here."

Gramps had nodded. "Yep. I've been expecting you. People talk and this is a small town. But there's not a word of truth to those stories. I'm not going crazy and there's no way in the world I'd ever hurt Max."

The Sheriff shrugged. "I believe you, Ben, but I have to do my job. Maybe a couple days in the mental hospital will help people sort out their concerns and that will be the end of it."

"Mental— what did he just say, hospital?' Max went cold with fear. His heart was pounding so hard he couldn't hear the rest of the conversation. He felt the heat rise in his face and his chest felt as though it would burst. Gramps turned to him, saying quietly, "Max, we'll both be fine. Please believe that. I'll be out soon and then I'll explain everything."

Explain everything about what Max had wondered. Before he could react, a tall, sad-looking woman in a gray skirt took his hand and told him he'd be fine, but he needed to go with her for a little while until his grandpa could get things figured out. Where were they going? His mind screamed he had to stay and take care of the farm. He couldn't just leave.

He pulled away from the woman and clung to Gramps. "Who'll take care of everything? Tell them I can stay. Please, Gramps, tell them."

"They have to make sure you are safe, Max. You're too young to stay alone. It's only for a little while. We'll be fine."

"I won't be alone! Please let me stay! Please." To no avail, his pleading fell on deaf ears, panic entered every nerve of Max's body; he could feel his muscles going rigid with fear.

Max was dragged into one of the cars, kicking and screaming. The last words Max heard his Gramps utter was that Millie, the housekeeper, would take care of the farm. It did little to ease Max's mind.

That was the last time Max had seen his Gramps. Several hours later, Max was dropped off at the steps of this old decaying building. He had no way of finding out about his Gramps or about his home.

Max had spent months trying to find a way to talk to his Gramps, but all his efforts led to dead ends. Max received several days of hard work and had been locked in more rooms then he could count whenever one of the teachers found him digging around for information. Even now, when Max thought about that final night, he felt a lump in his throat, and his eyes stung. Hadn't they said his

Gramps was crazy? At this moment, Max was pretty sure he was destined for the same fate as his Grandpa.

Thinking back, he remembered Gramps had spent a lot of time in the barn and in the shop; he often seemed distant and preoccupied. He even scolded Max once for entering the shop without knocking. The sight had been incredible— bats had formed a semi- circle around Gramps and he seemed to be conversing with them. Max couldn't be sure what had been going on since he was ordered out of there and it was never mentioned again. Gramps apologized —but what had he been up to?

Max rolled over on the hard cot as the hours slowly ticked by, he knew he wouldn't sleep tonight. He was too tired and upset; he'd already spent nearly six hours thinking daunting thoughts. Everyone else had gone to bed without bothering him, and the other boys were snoring and stinking up the room as usual. He definitely could not spend another moment in that room, he had to get some air. As he rolled out of his cot he wondered what Sam and Tracie thought of him. Would they still be his friends, or did they think he was going mad?

When Max knelt beside his crate, searching for his shoes in the dark, he was startled to hear Sam's whisper. "What's up Max? Can't you sleep? I can't either! What are you doing?"

"I thought I'd just walk a bit." Max whispered.

"Sounds good to me—can I come?"

"Sure, no problem," Max whispered.

The boys finished dressing and slipped out of the room without disturbing the others. They tiptoed along the corridor and down the steps, careful to avoid the creaking boards on steps nine, seven, and five. They reached the third floor and were headed down the long passageway when a door on the left suddenly flung open. They mashed themselves against the wall, hiding in the shadows.

A large shadowy figure left the room and turned in the opposite direction, carrying a light. The boys stood like statues, holding their breath. Suddenly the man swung around and turned the light on them. They were caught.

"Oh, no! We're in for it now," Sam muttered.

The tall, black-haired, dark-skinned man smiled, revealing perfect white teeth.

"Bailey! Are we glad it's you!" Max sighed with relief.

"What 'cha doing out an' about, you two? Come on – you best get outta the hall 'fore some growly ol' teach finds ya lurkin' about." Bailey Storm motioned the boys into his small, warm room.

Bailey was the janitor; one of the few nice adults at the orphanage, and a true friend to the three outcasts. Bailey had been left on the door of the orphanage over fifty-five years ago. He was an amazing man, everything he knew he learned on his own since all those years ago he was not allowed to attend classes. He had been taken under the wing of an ancient man by the name of Mr. Beavis who still roamed around the rooms occasionally. Mr. Beavis must be over a hundred years old by now since Bailey had told them that he was an old man back then. Bailey had stayed on after he grew up and had taken over Mr. Beavis's Janitorial job and worked here ever since.

He tried hard to make it a more bearable place for any of the kids willing to accept his friendship. His wide smile and massive size combined with the animated twinkle in his eye drew the three to him like a magnet. "I been missen you twos; aint seen ya in a bit where ya been keepin to?"

Max shrugged while forcing a half smile. "We've been up to the same old thing, homework and more homework. Of course, in my case there is also detention, which typically lasts for hours."

The boys entered a warm room which smelled of pipe tobacco and spicy aftershave; the old yellow clock on the small round table clicked and groaned with each new minute. The furnishings were meager and the room was small, yet comfortable. Four wooden rocking chairs with worn, dull pads sat in a half- circle around a warm rattling heater. His tiny bed seemed neither long nor wide enough for a man of Bailey's size. It was neatly made with a patched-up quilt on the top. The floor was kind of hard to make out since it was covered with old papers, little blobs of dust and an occasional article of clothing. Max didn't care; it was still the most comfortable room in the whole building.

Bailey motioned to a pair of rocking chairs. "Sit there and tell old Bailey what youse is doing roaming about dis ol' place. Youse ain't thinking about runnin out, is ya?" Bailey held up the flashlight he had carried to the hall and now shined it full into Max's face. "What in the world happened to you boy?"

Squinting at the light Max lowered his head "Had a disagreement with Lenny," he answered sheepishly.

"That don' look so good; hurts I'll bet." Bailey said putting the flashlight on the table next to him.

"It's not so bad now; hurts mostly if I laugh, but lately there isn't much to laugh at." Max grumbled feeling sorry for himself.

"So ya mad enough to try and escape or just anxious an can't sleep?"

"No, we just had to get some air," Max paused as Bailey eyed him keenly. Max squirmed a bit not wanting to lie but telling the whole story would certainly sound absurd to anyone else. After all he knew how it sounded to himself, let alone an adult who very possibly might think Max was heading off the deep end. "It's just so — well, stuffy in our room," Max opted for the lie.

"So ya say, but whatcha really doin?" Bailey could see straight through the fib. He remained calm, his brown eyes waiting patiently. He could read people better than anyone Max had ever met.

Sam blurted out the whole story before Max could stop him. Max fidgeted in his chair, wondering how Bailey would judge him.

When Sam finished, Bailey leaned back in his chair, pondering the tale. He took his pipe from the wobbly end table beside his bed and began to roll the tip around his lips. He seldom lit the pipe, but was often seen chewing on the end of it.

It seemed like hours before he spoke. Finally, he smiled and said, "It's jus the ghosts, boy. They's been hereabouts for many years. I seen em when ol' Bailey was jus a young sprout. I sees all the tricks they pull. Don't mean no harm, but they like to keep us live ones a-guessin."

"We have ghosts?" Max raised his eyebrows in disbelief.

Bailey nodded. "Stories told here say the two kids belonging to the man who owned this here house was kep' in a black room and throwed scraps and not let out to play or have any fun. Was told their momma was goin' insane and couldn't take the noise of the kids, so they was locked up and starved for love an' attention. They all dies young and haunted this here house and drove their momma to jump outta the attic winder. Their daddy fell into the ol' pond out back and drowned. That's why that ol' pond feels all cold an' dark, like death, ya know?"

Sam looked at him wide-eyed. "Have you seen these ghosts, Bailey?"

"Ya don' sees ghosts, boy. Ya sees the things they move, and hear the noise they make and notice the tricks they play. Why you think all the teachers ain't happy ta be here? You kids ain't suppose ta know about the ghosts, so best keep it to yourselfs. Boy, if this old house could talk jus thinks the stories you'd hear."

"Is there a painting of that family hanging in Mr. Crater's office? I think that must have been them. The man was the scariest looking guy I've ever seen and the kids were skinny and dirty, as was the woman. You don't suppose that could be them?" Max asked.

"Yep, I do believe at one time a very good likeness of them hanged on these old walls. I never knew exactly where. But if it is them, you can put a face to the ghosts now boy. They don' mean no harm. Hey, they helped ya with your schoolwork, din' they?"

"Yeah, I guess so. But I thought I was going crazy like my Gramps, that scared me."

Bailey waved his pipe in the air. "Max, that's jus pure nonsense. I'll bet your ol' Gramps weren't crazy neither. Maybe we's should try and find out about your ol' Gramps, huh? I could snoop around a little if ya wanted."

Max shook his head defeated. "Thanks, Bailey, but I tried and couldn't find anything, and that was after it first happened. The trail's cold by now."

"Maybe so, boy but ol' Bailey will see what he kin do for ya anyhow."

Bailey produced a bag of marshmallows and the three of them talked for several hours, sitting around the warm heater. By the time

Max and Sam left Bailey's room and sneaked back to their own beds, the night had nearly given way to dawn.

The boys collapsed on their cots and thankfully sleep embraced them snugly for the next few hours. Max fell into a deep slumber and had surprisingly pleasant dreams. All was quiet and cold; a scrim of ice covered the small window above his bed, inside and out. In the darkness beyond, a dark silhouette dove and darted through the night air.

Above them, in the dusty roof beam two glimmering, black eyes watched sedulously. Max awakened shortly before dawn, stretching his arms, he smiled as he remembered Bailey's words. Somehow the thought of ghosts haunting the building wasn't nearly as dreadful as losing his mind. He could deal with a ghost or two—what was the worst they could do?

The haunted eyes of the man in the painting made Max scoot down in the cot and cover himself tighter with the blanket. As he lay there thinking of all that had happened in the past couple days, Max drifted back to sleep.

CHAPTER FOUR

Still dreaming, smiling to himself, Max leapt up, startled as a pitcher of cold water sailed through the air and landed squarely in the middle of his chest and face. He gasped and sputtered from the shock of the cold water, wrath filling his body and mind. He sat up and shouted, "What in the —where did that come from?"

Lenny grinned. "Not sure, did you see anything, Rubin?"

Rubin looked at Gorfus with feigned surprise. "Not a thing."

Gorfus stifled a laugh. As Max sputtered and coughed up water, the terrible trio laughed uncontrollably and they headed for the door, it opened just as they reached for it; Sam stepped into the room his gaze took in the sight, he looked from one to the other, noticing the drowned rat appearance of his friend, and the gleeful smirks on the other three faces, the silence was overwhelming. The three boys backed up as Max came forward to stand beside Sam.

"These guys never learn, do they, Max?"

Max was in the process of drying off, while at the same time, glaring intently at his tormentors. What happened next was as baffling to Max as everything that had gone on for the previous two days. Without reason, Lenny turned to Gorfus and Rubin and hit each of them square on the nose. At the same time, Rubin and Gorfus spun and punched Lenny in the face. A total knockdown battle began. Max and Sam watched, absolutely bewildered as the three of them proceeded to beat on each other.

Realizing the situation could change at any moment, Max grabbed his clothes, motioned to Sam, and stepped into the hallway; Max was hopping on one leg trying to put on his pants as they went. Suddenly Max stopped dead in his tracks and stared at the floor.

Sam nudged him. "Hey, wasn't that the greatest thing you've ever seen? I was planning on pounding all three of those guys, but they saved me the trouble."

"Sam, something strange just happened again."

"Yeah, I know, those three imbeciles are still hitting each other. Listen to this will ya?" Sam pressed his ear up to the door. He could hear profanities being shouted and some thuds and crashes. Max grabbed his friend by the arm. "No I mean even more strange than that. I was thinking at the precise moment when they started to hit each other that I wanted them to do just that—hit each other. They did it exactly the way I thought it." Max stood stock still and looked at Sam as if expecting him to come up with a logical answer. The silence between them was as unrelenting as Max's irritation. It was annoying to Max that Sam didn't catch the significance.

Sam grinned. "So, you're saying you made that happen? Well if you did, then congratulations. Let me shake your hand." That was unquestionably not the answer Max was looking for. He wanted Sam to —well he didn't exactly know what he wanted. Unexpectedly he realized, a little embarrassed by his notion, he had no right to be upset with Sam when he had no idea what it was he wanted him to do about it either.

Sam stood there with his hand extended. Max shook it half-heartedly with a slight feeling of aggravation at his own feelings and said, "Don't you think any of this is seriously creepy?"

"Yeah, but lately, a lot of things have seemed peculiar. They seem to get more so with each passing day. Who knows, maybe by tomorrow you can find a way to think us out of this place?" Sam joked.

Max had to admit that Sam's nonchalant attitude was exactly what was needed to lessen the apprehension he was feeling.

"That would be nice. Not possible, but nice. I guess these odd things are simply unexplainable. It makes me feel a bit peculiar since it's mostly happening to me. It's like some kind of—" Max paused looking down at the buttons on his shirt that he was adjusting. "Well I don't know something seems to be watching over me and it reads my mind. It's just bizarre."

"You're right about that, but it is working in our favor, right?" Sam grinned. His enthusiasm was catching. Still a bit apprehensive Max smiled too. He nodded with the knowledge that whatever was coming next he would just have to deal with it. With a shrug of his bony shoulders he looked at Sam and asked, "Where have you been all morning while I was getting water poured all over me?"

"I got up early and went down to talk to Bailey. Then I decided I'd better wake you up and that's when I came back. Which one of those guys threw the water on you?"

"I don't know. I was still sleeping," Max snarled.

"Well, however it worked, I hope you can tell them to beat each other up more often."

The two boys hurried downstairs to breakfast, anxious to tell Tracie about all the excitement. She was sitting at the table waiting for them when they arrived. After hearing the story, she laughed and gave Max a high five. "Way to go! The three goons deserve every punch they landed on each other."

As the three of them ate their hot cereal, Tracie stopped midway to her mouth with her spoon, deep in thought, a peculiar look on her face.

"What are you thinking, Tracie?" Max asked.

"I think you have a new friend in this school and I believe it's one of the ghosts of the kids who used to live here. I read an article in an old newspaper a long time ago that told about this place being haunted. It was always hushed and explained away, but I believe that kind of thing can happen."

"That's funny," Sam told her. "Last night we talked to Bailey and he said the same thing."

"We couldn't figure out why these ghosts would want to bother with me." Max said. "What interest would they have in me—and why now? We never even knew they existed before now."

Sam shrugged. "Bailey did say he thought they were good kids, just bad circumstances. Maybe they somehow know you're a good kid too and they can also see how cruel the others are to you. Suppose it's their way of helping you out."

Tracie nodded. "You know, they can probably watch everything we do without our knowledge. Maybe they've been watching you for a long time."

"I don't know, I'm tired of thinking about this, it's making me edgy." Max bit his lower lip; he looked down at his hands and began to methodically pick at the still fresh scab he had obtained from his nose dive earlier in the week.

He looked up just in time to see Lenny and his friends enter the room, maybe they were still friends. Their clothing untidy, their faces marked and bruised. Max looked at Sam and grinned. Lenny held a bloody handkerchief under his nose and the three of them were still snapping at each other. The room grew silent as the three boys found a table and began eating their meal. The rest of the students whispered and watched.

Max thought this would be a good time to make his exit; he stood to leave, with Sam and Tracie at his side. They allowed themselves one last look toward the three black and blue buddies. They sniggered as they left the room to arrive at their first class of the morning.

The room was empty so they took their seats and chatted softly to one another. It was quiet for a while until the others started filtering in.

Mrs. R. had heard about the scuffle of her three favorite students and the rumor that Max had something to do with it; she decided it was a good day to make him squirm. As class began, she called on him for every menial task that she could think of. Then she humiliated him by asking him to review the class discussion that had taken place while he was busy handing out papers, wiping the chalkboards, sharpening pencils, picking up garbage, and putting books onto the shelves in alphabetical order. Max stared blankly at her.

When she saw the puzzled look planted firmly on his face, she shouted, "Well, Mr. Morgan, it appears you're too busy being a bully to pay attention. Perhaps you need a rest. Stand in the corner now,

Mr. Morgan, and don't move until I tell you to. You may even, if you wish, take your little nap."

Max listened to the giggles of his classmates as he rose to go to the corner.

The look on Tracie's face told him she was furious. She snapped, "You know, Mrs. Rosenblam, if you'd done your own lousy little chores, Max could have concentrated on your lesson."

Mrs. Rosenblam turned around, looking as though someone had slapped her. This time she directed her outrage at Tracie. "Miss Miller, you have a bad habit of sticking your nose in where it doesn't belong."

Tracie looked as shocked as everyone else in the room that she had spoken up in Max's defense. This was the first time she had ever opened her mouth to a teacher.

"Maybe you'd like to stand in the adjacent corner and rest your mouth, Miss Miller. NOW!"

Max felt his face enflame with anger. At the same time, he saw tears of embarrassment running down Tracie's cheeks. She walked to the front of the room, all eyes on her now, and stood across from Max.

As Mrs. Rosenblam turned back to the other students, the erasers flew off the ledge of the chalkboard and landed on the floor next to Max's feet. His look of surprise was only surpassed by Mrs. Rosemblam's red-faced eye-bulging anger. With all eyes on him, he knew he should say something in his defense, but for the life of him, he couldn't even manage a groan.

Mrs. Rosenblam approached him, a look of rage fixed on her face. "Well, well, Mr. Morgan, I see you want to show off your total disregard for authority to the whole class. I wonder if a few hours of cleaning up and organizing the library might help your penchant for trouble-making, hmm?"

The class laughed and cheered as she led him by the scruff of the shirt out the door and into the library— well, what they called the library. It was a small, dusty, dark room with books, papers, files, and other items scattered on the chairs and floor. None of the two hundred or so books were on the shelves, since the shelves were falling down and broken.

"This, Mr. Morgan, will keep you busy the rest of the day and well into the night. I'll come and get you when I feel you've been here long enough. Do NOT leave. I want all these books put on the shelves in alphabetical order. Do I make myself clear? You do know what alphabetical order is, don't you?" With a nasty little sneer, Mrs. Rosenblam slammed the door, sending a poof of dust into the air.

Max sat back on a chair, considering his options. A large, gray spider crawled across his foot and scurried off under a stack of papers. His first thought was to leave this horrible place and never look back, but since he couldn't manage that— his next option was to get some well-deserved rest. He knew Mrs. Rosenblam would keep him locked away until his eighteenth birthday if he didn't follow her orders.

"I didn't knock those erasers off the ledge, I was simply thinking of throwing them at her," he growled to no one in particular. He felt a kinship to the little gray spider now climbing up the side of the bookcase. The dark day and the dirty window made it hard for Max to see the full extent of the filth and disarray of the room before him.

Max went to the window and looked out over the grounds which were as murky as he felt. He noted something different out there today, a bright oblong glow made him squint. The light moved closer to the window, and then it shot off at extreme speed up into the sky. "Mm, wonder what that was?" He moved the stack of books away from the window to allow more light, and then pulled at the tattered, black, dusty shade, opening it full to expose the window. With a crash, the shade fell to the floor in a cloud of dust and cobwebs. The dim light filtering in gave him a better view of the mess surrounding him.

The one nice thing about being locked in this room was that he was alone without the glances and grimaces from the other kids. Max began to wonder as he looked around just how many six and eight legged critters inhabited this grubby area.

Starting in the farthest corner, Max began stacking the books into piles on the floor. He looked around for a broom, or something that resembled a broom, but found only a small dirty rag. He shook out the rag and began wiping down books.

Hours later, he had all the books in several stacks and for the most part clean. "Now for the shelves," he said looking over to where he'd last seen the spider.

Max wondered how he was supposed to fix the shelves without a hammer, or nails, or any other tools. He had learned fairly young how to repair and build things. Gramps had told him it was important to learn those skills that would help him become more self sufficient. Max hadn't cared what the reason; he just enjoyed creating something out of nothing. This would qualify as nothing, yet he had no resources to enable him to fix the shelves.

He sighed, realizing he was far from getting this ghastly job done. He was hungry and tired, his eyes and nose were full of dust, his hair full of cobwebs. Frustration welled up inside him. As he was crossing the room to the door to see if it was locked, someone pounded on the door, followed by the rattling of the door knob.

Sam shot through the door and quickly shut it. "Wow, I've had a time trying to sneak away to check on ya. It always seemed like someone was watching me. How ya doing? This place is trashed. Here, I brought you half my stale bologna and pickle sandwich."

"Thanks. I'm so hungry, even this looks good."

"Yeah, it wasn't too bad. We've had much worse. Oh, here's some water." Sam produced a well-worn milk carton. Max knew it couldn't have been today's, as it was rare they got milk. "So how did you get in here? I thought the old bag locked the door."

"Oh, yeah, she locked it, but it was no problem." Sam held up a twisted, bent wire. "Sometimes knowing how to pick locks comes in handy." Sam smiled a mischievous grin showing straight white teeth and deep dimples. His cocoa brown eyes twinkled.

"That's for sure, especially around here, you need to teach me how since I'm the one usually locked away somewhere."

Sam nodded, "yeah one of these days I'll do that."

"I need to learn how before they lock me away in a real horrible place." Max mumbled through a mouth full of dry sandwich. Quickly he devoured the skimpy meal looked at Sam and said. "This crazy woman is making me fall so far behind in my work. Do you think you could find a way to sneak me my math book and papers, maybe stuff them under the door?"

Sam wandered around taking in all of the disarray; he walked to the window and peered out. "Good idea. You could use this time to get your homework done; you never know how long she'll keep you here. Do you expect you'll have to stay here if you don't get finished?"

Max nodded, "Yeah, no doubt about that. I don't see how I can do anymore arranging here." He flung a book across the room. "Maybe I'll just stay here for the next few years, at least its quiet."

They talked a bit more, before Sam said, "I better go before I get sent to a dirty room to clean up someone else's mess." Grinning at Sam's obvious jest, Max thanked him and Sam snuck back out the door as quickly as he'd entered.

Max sat on the dirty floor to digest his lunch, which had been better then most days. The bologna was halfway fresh and the bread, although dry, had shown very little mold. His stomach quieted, his spirits lifted, he thought through his next task. How was he supposed to get any books to stay on shelves that were falling down and broken?

Clean, but how?

CHAPTER FIVE

Max rubbed his eyes. He felt better— the severe hunger pains were gone, the nagging wish for something more to eat was always with him; he was used to that, but he was tired of everything else. It seemed he was always in trouble, yet seldom was it his fault. As he sat looking at the work in front of him, his imagination ran wild, he stifled a yawn.

A booming voice from the other side of the door broke the silence. "Here it is; have fun. See ya tonight, maybe." The math book, paper and pencil were shoved under the space between the floor and the door.

"Thanks Sam," Max jumped up retrieving his school work then returned to the bare spot on the floor. He lay back opting to do a little of the math now and save the cleaning for later.

Page after page, he flew through the assignments; the answers came to him faster and more correctly then ever before. Maybe it was the peacefulness of the room or maybe it was his hard- headed determination to succeed. Whatever the reason, he smiled at his efforts; he had finished all three chapters. At the end of the assignment he sat back to rest for a few minutes. He had no idea when or even if, anyone would let him out of the library so he may as well rest.

Max closed his eyes and immediately fell into a strange dream. He was helping an old woman pull spiders from her hair, but more spiders kept crawling out. He would pull them, and then more would come. He'd just finished when a large dog came out of the closet and offered Max his bone. As he reached out to take the bone, Max realized it was a human arm bone, with the hand and fingers still attached. They grabbed at him while the dog said, "Drink your milk or there will be no more cookies."

Suddenly, the big mushroom-like face of his math teacher, Mr. Brittle, popped into his head and told him to copy down all numbers known to man and be sure and put a cherry on top. Max felt as though he were swishing through a culvert filled with water. He couldn't breathe or open his eyes. He realized he was being sucked down to the bottom of a large cold lake. Suddenly he was holding the head of a woman, her body dangled in mid –air; he was biting her neck, a trickle of blood appeared and her screams woke him.

With a gasp, Max sat straight up, looking around. A red imprint from his pencil was tattooed on his forehead. He rubbed his eyes and for a moment he had no idea where he was. Then suddenly, the surroundings became familiar. How long had he slept? A bit of light still showed through the window; he knew it was no later than four-thirty. There were no sounds beyond the door; class was out.

The sound of a key scraping the locked door made Max jump up and grab his book and assignment. The door burst open and there stood the hideous Mrs. Rosenblam. "Yuck, what a sight to wake up to!" She looked as though she had read his thoughts; she pursed her thin lips as though she'd eaten a nasty-tasting morsel. As she looked around, the sour look vanished; it was replaced by disbelief and awe. Max followed her stare; he too was struck with awe. The room looked as though an army of cleaning ladies had marched through, leaving every piece of furniture repaired, every book in its place, and all dust and cobwebs gone.

Mrs. Rosenblam coughed, evidently at a loss for words. Max thought this would be the best time to make his escape. He backed out slowly, still confused as to how the room had gotten so clean. He raced down the hall and up the stairs, up the next flight, and the next. He was out of breath and out of his mind with panic. "How did it happen? Was he still dreaming?" He had to find Sam and tell him about it. As he rounded the corner to the fourth set of stairs, Max ran into Lenny head-on, knocking them both off their feet, sending them crashing to the floor.

Max sat up bemused. Lenny screamed at him, shouting and swearing, but Max had no time to listen. He jumped up, rubbed the sore spot on his head and sprinted up the stairs with Lenny's insults trailing behind. Breathless and sore, Max flung open the door to his dorm room and shouted, "Sam I have to talk to you right now!"

Sam looked up from his book, startled by the sudden loud outburst. "What's up, Max?"

Max bent over in an effort to gain his composure and his breath. "I was just in the library and… well…"

Sam ushered him over to the cot, sat Max down and pulled up a crate and sat down in front of him. "Now, slow down and catch your breath."

"The library was clean," Max blurted out.

"Good job! You got it all done."

Max shook his head. "Yes and no. I did my math and then fell asleep shortly after you left. When I woke up Mrs.Rosenblam opened the door. The room was spotless and completely organized. You saw how bad it was. No way did I do all that!"

Sam thought for a moment. "Wow! Do you think it was the ghosts?"

"I'm not sure, but I do know I didn't finish that room."

"Wow, just think what this could mean. You could get sent to all of the other rooms to clean while avoiding class and take a nap and poof the chore is done."

"Speak for yourself. I'm the one at the center of all this madness and I'm not so sure I like it."

Sam could see Max was concerned and Sam's attempt to make him feel better was a bit lame. "Sorry, Max, I know this is spooky but whoever has been helping you has been doing things for the better. It might work to your advantage."

"Well, yeah, I guess, I'm not sure how I feel. I think we should do some digging around and see what more we can find out about these ghosts."

Sam tossed his book aside. "Let's go talk to Bailey again; I bet he knows more than he told us."

"Tonight then, after we eat."

Between all the excitement in the library and Max relaying the story to Sam, the boys had only ten minutes before dinner. They stored their books on the beds and put on sweaters to avoid the chill that seeped into the building.

This time of night, when the teachers left, the heat was turned down and the temperature dropped into the low fifties. As they walked downstairs to the cafeteria, Lenny was waiting at the bottom of the steps with a smug look on his face.

Mrs. Rosenblam stepped around the corner, hands on her hips. "Mr. Morgan, you seem to have no consideration for anyone but yourself and your little friend here," she gestured toward Sam.

Sam and Max looked at each other, confused.

"Look at this young boy you ran into and knocked down—look what you did to him!" Mrs. Rosenblam turned Lenny's face so they could see the remnants of his bloody nose.

"I didn't mean to run into him. He was coming down when I was going up and we bumped into each other and besides look what he did to me." Max said pointing to his black and blue face.

Lenny whined, "You ran into me. I was walking when you ran up the stairs into me."

"You probably should watch where you are walking then," Sam growled.

"You may go and eat, Mr. Springfield. This does not concern you," Mrs. Rosenblam said through clenched teeth.

"If it concerns Max, it concerns me."

"Sam, it's ok. Don't get in trouble over this. I'll be okay. Go ahead and eat," Max whispered.

After directing an annoyed glance at Lenny, Sam grudgingly set off for the dinner line. Behind them Sam mimed a few humorous gestures leaving Max trying not to laugh. He tried to keep his attention focused on the two in front of him.

"I think you need to be accountable for your behavior, Mr. Morgan. I am going to write a note to Mr. Crater, and he can decide your punishment. At this time, you will apologize to this nice young man for your careless behavior."

"Sorry," Max growled, scowling at both of them.

"Very well then; that is the best I'm sure you can do with an attitude such as yours. You both may go eat. I will take this to Mr. Crater and you will be hearing from him soon."

Max walked away, wishing the writing would disappear from the paper just as his note in math had done. Max had grown increasingly despondent due to the past several confusing events, this episode only succeeded in heightening his agitation.

New Information

CHAPTER SIX

Dinner was as disgusting as usual, but everyone shoveled down the food to keep from feeling hunger pangs all night long. Max found it difficult to control his gloomy thoughts, striking up a cheery conversation just wouldn't do. Instead he talked about the trouble he was going to be in when Mr. Crater heard the story that Mrs. Rosenblam was going to tell, of course it would be Lenny's version. Sam and Tracie agreed he'd be in hot water when Mr. Crater read the note.

Tracie thought he should tell Mr. Crater about Mrs. Rosenblam's flaws, but Max knew that was fruitless. No one would believe him. Mr. Crater already thought he was a pampered little pain who needed to learn to follow the rules. Mr. Crater actually showed no favoritism— he hated all the kids equally.

"You know if you really think about it I guess I am to blame. I was after all running in the halls and I did run into him, if it were anyone else I would feel bad." Max smiled, "I'll take my punishment and appreciate that he deserved it." Max nodded to himself a smidgen of a self- indulgent feeling hung over him. He paused then looked at Tracie.

"Sam and I are going to sneak down and see what else Bailey might know about the ghosts and see if he actually found anything out about Gramps. Do you want to meet us down there?" Max asked.

Tracie frowned, "I would like to, but"— she paused, "Max you need to be very careful. You know how these teachers feel about sneaking around digging for information on anything outside these walls," she warned.

"I know we'll be careful; besides Bailey's doing most of the probing we're just checking back with him. That's all." Max promised.

Tracie nodded but refused to accompany them this time, insisting she had a huge pile of homework that was steadily building up on her. The boys said good-bye and headed back upstairs to their room. They couldn't visit Bailey's room while any students or teachers roamed the halls, or they'd risk getting Bailey in trouble too, so they sat on the floor working on as much homework as possible waiting for time to pass. Max had gotten his math done and Sam was still far behind so he copied from Max's paper. Later when their roommates entered, the two boys crawled under their blankets and feigned deep sleep.

It seemed like hours had passed; the room was engulfed in darkness, Max and Sam could tell by the snoring that their roommates were asleep. They quietly crawled out from under the covers and headed for the door, peering into the dimly lit hallway. No one was in sight; they stepped out and headed downstairs slowly, quietly carrying their shoes.

They moved past old watchdog Twill's room, stepping gingerly as they knew she was a light sleeper and would hear them if they made even the slightest noise. Suddenly a huge black figure descended on them from above. They ducked, plastering their bodies flat against the wall, at the top of the staircase.

"What was that?" whispered Sam.

"I'm not sure, but I think it might have been the bat I saw the other day. You know the one I told you about."

"It almost made me yell at it, which probably would have woken everyone causing us to get caught!" Sam whispered.

The stairs below them creaked a warning; someone had just placed a foot on the bottom step. The boys backed around the corner into the shadows and held their breath; they could hear each step groan with the weight of the dark, looming body. The shuffle of the tired, old feet told them it was Mrs. Twill; she practically dragged her feet when she walked. The distinct smell of cat urine made both boys instinctively plug their noses. They all suspected Mrs. Twill of having a cat due to the foul smell that followed her, yet no cat had ever been seen.

Standing still and trying not to breathe, the boys waited until she entered her room and closed the door behind her.

"Whew, that was close," Max whispered. "If we hadn't stopped when that bat flew by, we would have been caught."

"Do you think it was trying to warn us?" Sam whispered.

Max nodded. "It seems that way. Hard to say; it shows up at some pretty strange times."

Sam stepped out from against the wall. "I'm surprised Mrs. Twill didn't sniff us out, she has a reputation of being able to smell kids. Do you think that's true or just a rumor?"

Max groaned while he fanned the air with his hand, "I don't know, but I can sure smell her."

"Yeah, no kidding," Sam agreed.

"Come on; let's get going before we get caught."

The light was on under the door of Bailey's room. They knocked lightly on the door and waited; no answer. They tapped louder and whispered his name. "Bailey, are you there?" They heard papers rustling, the lock turned, and the door opened. Bailey peered out at them with a wide smile on his clean- shaven face.

"Well, well, look what the ol' cat dragged in! Come in, come in. I been thinking abouts you two boys and wanten to give ya some news. Seems it's kinda hard gettin past the cranky ol' teachers. Sit down." He motioned toward the two rocking chairs across from him.

Max settled his tired body back onto the familiar worn chair and breathed a relaxing sigh. "We almost got caught by Mrs. Twill. She was downstairs and we didn't know it."

"You boys ought not be wanderin around, that Mrs. Twill will chew ya up and spit ya out she will." Bailey said shaking his head.

"Bailey, are there bats in this place that are big and fat and have green eyes?" Sam asked on the heels of Max's prior comment.

"Bats, you say?" He looked at Max. "I can't says I seen any green-eyed bats in the builden', but I sure seen some of them fellers outside. No green eyes, though I don think, can't say as I ever got close enough to look at their eyes."

Max cleared his throat, and said, "I've seen this one before, but tonight was the first time Sam saw it. We think it was trying to warn us that it wasn't safe to go any further down the hall." Max had left out the bat and bird part of his story the last time he talked with Bailey, so he relayed the story of the extrasensory conversation with the bat.

Bailey seemed interested. "I's not so sure about bats, fellers. Things that fly about gives ol' Bailey the creeps."

Max nodded. "It did me too at first, back home at the farm we had several hanging around. At first I was kind of freaked by them but they meant no harm they just hung around in the day and flew around at night— but anyway this one in the school is helpful and it talks to me so—" Max gulped, and the rest of his statement trailed off into oblivion. He realized how ridiculous that just sounded.

"Could jus' be some critters that live here and maybe with all that's goin' on you imagined em speakin' to ya," Bailey said.

Max said nothing; he didn't agree, but he kept it to himself. After they finished dissecting that and the other news going on around school, Bailey produced a large stack of newspapers. "I told you I'd find out what I could about your Gramps, Max, and here's a good start. I hope you can decipher somthin outa these. It wasn't easy gettin it, so don' go telling no one."

"Wow, this is great Bailey. Thanks." Smiling, Max took the papers, leaned back in the chair, and started looking through them. He was so intent on finding out about his Gramps he almost forgot Sam and Bailey were in the room. The silence caused him to look up from the stack. His two friends had been watching with interest while his sole concentration had been on the newspapers.

Max looked awkwardly at them. "Oh, I'm sorry; guess I got carried away. What we really came up to talk about were the ghosts and what it is they actually do and if you think they can be brought about so we can talk with them."

"They seem to have taken a real liking to Max," Sam said.

"Yeah and I don't know what I did to deserve their help." The boys relayed the latest stories of the library and the other incidents that seemingly must have been done by something other than a human.

When they finished, Bailey just nodded and said, "Sounds kinda like them there ghosts."

"What other types of things have you known these ghosts to do?" Sam asked, looking over at Max, who was half- heartedly listening. His true attention was on the stack of papers Bailey had given him. Sam reached his foot out and tapped Max on the leg. Max looked up with an apologetic look and set the papers aside on the little table.

Bailey chuckled and cleared his throat. "I can tells ya the stuff that has been done is mostly things bein' moved to different places, missin' school books, hot water runnin' cold and vice versa. Alls these strange sounds at night done frightened away the teachers. Theys would spend the night and leave on the weekends, now they waste no time getting outta heres after each day's work."

It was obvious to Max that the occurrences Bailey described weren't nearly as obvious as the events happening around Max. The three talked until early morning. The boys finally bid Bailey good night sometime after two a.m. Max carried the papers to his room. His eagerness to look through them made him ache to flip on the light and start his search, yet he knew he would be in deep trouble if he woke his roommates. Ignoring his yearning, they flopped into their cots fully dressed. It didn't take long before they were fast asleep.

Morning brought with it a cold dreary wetness that muddied the grounds. Purple gray clouds hung low over the foul building. The dingy window steamed over with a wet haze. Max and Sam, already dressed, scurried out of the room before the gruesome threesome started the morning ritual of harassing Max and infuriating Sam.

"I hope I can stay awake in class today. These late nights are killing me." Max yawned.

"Me too," Sam yawned back.

They trudged through the corridors towards the cafeteria. Tracie was already there studying, looking as though she had been there all night. She looked up from her book and smiled a lopsided grin, "Hey, how was the evening at Bailey's?"

Max grinned while talking between bites of toast. "Pretty good, I guess. We really don't know much more than we did before. Bailey said the ghosts would usually just misplace people's stuff and change hot and cold water, make strange noises in the night and things such as that. They definitely didn't do homework, cause fights, and clean libraries."

Sam shook his head not in the least convinced that a ghost had done any of this.

Max sat up and brightened a little. "I did get a pile of papers that have some articles about my Grandpa though. We were so busy talking last night that I never got a chance to look through them."

Tracie smiled and leaned forward looking at Max as though he had just offered her a box of chocolates. "Wow, Bailey found some stuff out about your Grandpa, that's great!" Tracie smiled and clapped her hands.

Max nodded and looked strangely at Tracie's excited face. "I would guess by the look on your face you probably want to help me look through the papers?"

"We'll help you if you want us too," Sam said,

"Sure, we can help you sort through the papers, if you want our help." Tracie smiled, acting indifferent. "Actually," she giggled "you couldn't keep us away."

Max smiled with the knowledge that soon he might know what had become of his Gramps. He got the biggest grin that his friend's excitement was even greater than his own. He didn't want to get his hopes up too high, for fear they might not lead to anything more then he already knew. "Your help would be great. Maybe it won't take all night to sort through them." Max said drowsily, trying to stifle a yawn behind his hand.

Tracie leaned forward, looked around the room making sure no one could hear her, and whispered. "The hard part is finding a place where we should meet. We need a place where no one will find us. We also need to wait until everyone is asleep, including snoopy old Mrs. Twill."

"We could sneak down to the library, now that Max cleaned it up so nicely for us." Sam said grinning.

They all laughed, looking up in time to see Mr. Crater striding toward them with a paper in his hand. "Oh no, it's Mr. Crater. I'm in trouble now. He's going to punish me for running into Lenny yesterday."

Looking at the three with extreme contempt in his eyes, Mr. Crater slammed the paper on the table while looking at Max.

"This was in the hall. Has your name on it, Morgan. Keep our school clean, use the trash can."

After he stalked off, Max picked up the paper. The only writing on it was a scribbled name at the beginning of the page that read, *Max Morgan*. The rest was blank. It appeared to be Mrs. Rosenblam's scribbled writing. Had she forgotten to write the rest of the complaint, or had it vanished like the writing on the paper in math class. It seemed as though Sam had read Max's mind. "Your ghosts again I assume?"

"Something similar to that, I suppose. Thanks to whoever helped me out of this one." Max looked up to the ceiling and smiled. Sam grabbed the paper out of Max's hand looking at Max's scribbled name on the page. Shrugging he handed it back to Max who took one more glance and there it was clear and precise: ***"You're Welcome."*** Something caught in Max's throat and he thrust the paper back to

Sam who took it saying "yeah, I know its Mrs. Rosenblam's writing with your name."

Max shook the paper "No, look at the— *You're Welcome.*"

"The what?" Sam asked looking at the paper again, "You're mad." Sam said pushing the paper back to Max.

Max looked at the paper. It had happened again, all that remained there in black ink was his name.

"Max there's no doubt that something or someone is keeping you out of trouble, I'm just guessing, but I believe there is much more to it then we think," Sam said.

Max nodded. Completely stumped he wasn't going to even press the point of the "you're welcome." He didn't have the energy; he actually had nothing more to add so he just looked at Sam and Tracie, a confused self-conscious smile creased his mouth.

"Something very wacky is going on," Tracie said, thinking out loud. They came to the agreement that they would meet around ten p.m. in the library

After the three emptied their hardly-touched meal into the appropriate place, they made their way to the first class.

Standing in the doorway of her class room was the insidious Mrs. Rosenblam. Promptly, and with malice in her voice she instructed Max to clean up several large sticky wads of gum, which had somehow attached themselves to the erasers, which had in turn attached themselves to the windows. Unpleasant as it was he suffered through and made no comments for fear that he may find himself in even a worse predicament.

Fortunately for Max that was the worst part of the day. The rest of the day dashed by probably due to the lack of attention Max gave to the teachers. He sat there numb and oblivious throughout the day.

When the bell signaled school was out to relieve Max from a dragging day, he found a new excitement filling his body. He felt an eagerness he hadn't felt in a long while.

Max, Sam and Tracie hurried through their meal as though it where actually edible. Then they rushed to their rooms and tried to get as much schoolwork done as they could to avoid falling behind. Outside, the darkness grew blacker while the chill in the air seeped in; the trio flopped onto their cots and feigned sleep until a stillness penetrated the building.

Tracie had agreed since she had a watch, she would tap lightly on the boys' door at ten. Her roommates were not as mean as Max's. They were younger and mostly just ignored her, sometimes making rude remarks, but mostly treating her like they were better than her. Tracie knew she would not have a chance to fall asleep due to Arabeth's nightly ritual of mud masks, moisture packs, etc. These habits of hers rarely concluded before nine or so. Tracie wondered what the prim little thing would do when she ran out of her supplies. She doubted anyone would purchase them for her.

Ten o'clock approached at a snail's pace. Tracie left the warmth of her cot, grabbed a couple of sweaters, and snuck out into the hall. She walked as quietly as the old wood floor would allow, all the while keeping her eyes and ears open for anyone who might still be awake. She approached the boys' room and knocked as lightly on the door as she could to avoid waking all of them.

Max and Sam had not fallen asleep for fear they would not wake up; they heard her light tapping on the door. Together they grabbed their shoes and sweaters, leaving the dark, rancid smelling room.

Once they were out in the corridor, the three made their way down the hall, then slowly down the groaning staircase. They tried to be as quiet and careful as they could. The large stack of papers in Max's and Sam's hands rustled softly. They made it to the library, ducked inside and quietly shut the door.

"Don't light the candle yet," Tracie whispered taking off her extra sweater, she tucked it under the space between the floor and the door so that the light could not be seen from the hall. She then reached over and lit the candle they had borrowed the night before from Bailey. Even with the flame, it was dark and spooky in the library. Max could hardly contain his excitement. Having waited this long, he really hoped to find something out about his Gramps.

"Wow, someone really cleaned this old place," Sam whispered.

"See what I was talking about being all clean and repaired? No one even thanked me either." Max faked indignation and they laughed.

The excitement in the air was contagious. Tracie squealed with delight; the twinkle in her brown eyes told the boys she could hardly wait. She set to work finding a spot to sit. Carefully sitting down on the floor in the back corner they formed a circle and began pouring through the papers. There was not much talk for the first twenty minutes or so. The articles were not very informative at first, and then the lies that had been published jumped from the pages, hitting Max full throttle with a feeling of rage and scandal.

The headline at the top with a full page devoted to pure nonsense read: ***"Elderly man accused of child neglect and possible mental impairment"***.

Grandfather endangers young boy while participating in cult worship; witnesses say boy tied up in garage, left for days while grandfather conjured evil spirits.

The more the three read on, the more they began to believe someone was completely out of their minds, and it was not Max's Gramps or Max.

"Listen to this," Sam said incredulously. *"I just can't believe that a nice old man would whip this boy every night and lock him in the cupboard of the old farmhouse, but that's what we witnessed, said a good source who was close to the family, Mrs. Eggheart."*

"Who the heck is Mrs. Eggheart?" growled Max, "and for that matter, what is she talking about?"

"Oh, look how cute you were," Tracie said. The picture showed Max and the tall lady in the gray skirt who had taken Max from his home. Max was much shorter and his bones had far more meat on them versus the current withered version. Max frowned at the picture. "It seems like a lifetime since then."

As Max looked at the picture in the paper the memories came flooding back to him. The aloof attitude of the woman who had led him to the car, her dark stare had been unwavering. Even now, looking at her picture, Max felt her gaze pierce his heart. She spoke very little on the long ride. Max had been frantic; needing someone to talk to him; she had just sat there as though she were an inanimate object. Occasionally a set of crystal blue eyes appeared in the rear view mirror and had locked onto Max's fearful ones; the drivers' gaze had actually calmed him. Max had sensed new comfort and relaxed with a glance every now and again into the mirror. Max wondered now as he reflected back on that night who those eyes had belonged to. Suddenly his stomach did a great gurgle and a leap as he recalled the sickening sweet odor that night in the car. Whatever it had been it was still fresh in his mind, he memorized vividly how it had made him green with nausea.

Max took a deep breath and wiped away the past memories determined to embrace the new information they were filing through.

"Whoa, Max, check this out." Sam handed over the paper that read: "*Ben Morgan, arrested on charges of child endangerment and devil worshipping, was sent to Craver Mental Hospital for psychological evaluation from where he later escaped. No one knows where he went or even how he escaped. Witnesses say Mr. Morgan was in a padded, locked cell with guards standing by when he just disappeared. If anyone knows anything of his disappearance, please contact...*"

Max skipped through to the end. "He is considered very dangerous and deranged."

"DANGEROUS AND DERANGED?! What are they thinking? This is crazy I can't believe any of this actually got published in a newspaper," Max blurted angrily.

"Do you recognize any of the names of the so-called witnesses?" Tracie's eyes bore into him expecting an answer. Max had always had nothing but good things to say about his Gramps; his friends knew these articles were wrong. Max thought so hard his head ached and his stomach churned. "Not so far. They are all people I've never heard of."

"Do you think your Gramps may have been involved in, well, you know, something illegal?" Sam asked.

"No, he never associated with anyone. He always just worked hard; we both did. We were almost always together. I would have known if he was up to something dangerous or wrong. The only time he was off by himself was when he was in his machine shop. He never allowed me in his shop, but that was because he said sometimes people needed a place just for themselves."

"Listen to this!" Tracie was fascinated and amazed as she continued to read: "*Authorities say Ben Morgan had been institutionalized and escaped while his young grandson, Max, was missing; both of their whereabouts are unknown. The family housekeeper, Millie, states that she will continue to search for answers about her friend Ben and little Max.*"

Millie. Short, chunky Millie who had been the closest thing to a grandmother Max had. She was a dear old friend of his Gramps' and had been with them for many years. She lived a few yards behind the main house in a little cottage. She had no family, so she doted on Ben and Max constantly. She was always bustling around, cooking, cleaning, and humming to herself.

Max remembered one time in particular he wanted to play a trick on her. He worked the better part of the afternoon trying to catch a rattlesnake without getting bit and put it in a jar. He tightened the lid securely and placed it in the refrigerator. He will never forget when he got back in from working and sat down to eat with a ravenous appetite, he complimented Millie on how good dinner had been.

Millie had thanked him for the wonderful fresh meat. Max had looked confused at first until Millie held up the old mayonnaise jar that the snake had been in. Max remembered a sick feeling; he ate a snake. He'd heard other people say they had eaten snake, but he never planned on being one of them. The laughter that day in the kitchen after he had turned a pasty color came back to him now and he grinned.

"Max are you listening to me or not?" Tracie whispered as loudly as she dare.

Max's mind returned back to present, yet still he spoke as if he were in a trance, a look of perplexity planted firmly on his motionless face.

"She was like my grandma I never had. I wonder if she is still at the farm." Max's faraway look was of speculation.

Tracie broke the silence again her insistence grew as she had not gotten Max's full attention; her impatience amplified, she grabbed his arm and shook it. "Did you hear what I said? They say you were MISSING;" she shouted the last word into his seemingly impenetrability brain. "This is the more recent edition of the *Information Chronicle.* It's dated three months after the first one came out, three months after you were brought here."

Tracie was trying to get Max to see the whole picture. Tracie watched Max; the light finally came on, "Hey, they brought me here.

What do they mean, missing?" He looked from one to the other of them. "What do you think that means?" He frowned.

"I think," Sam pondered, "someone has made a very big mess out of your life, my friend."

"Yeah," Tracie agreed, "something just doesn't add up when you look at these articles. Maybe Ben had enemies who may have set him up or something?"

"I just don't think he made any enemies who would do something like this." Max said pausing to read the article again. "I mean sure there were a few people that Gramps didn't always get along with for whatever reason, but it wasn't bad enough for them to spread rumors and cause us trouble."

"Maybe the old lady uh….. What did you say her name was? Oh yeah, Millie, set him up so she could take the farm." Sam suggested.

"No way," Max laughed. "That's ridiculous. She was our friend. She was happy the way it was. I have never heard of any of these witnesses referred to in these articles." Max said holding up the newspaper. This had to be set up by someone. What about this cult worshipping, beating me, and locking me up? None of our friends would say anything like that because they know it's not true. The sheriff that came out to our place that night was our friend. He said he knew Gramps had done nothing wrong but he had to do his job and follow up on complaints. I just wonder who complained and why."

Sam stared off into the darkness; his mind was searching for some sort of logic. "There really isn't much more we can do to find out what is going on unless—?"

"We should go back and talk to Bailey. He's the only friend we have that can help us," Max said with a hint of regret in his voice. He realized he had ignored Sam and now he looked over at Sam. "Unless what"?

Sam nodded and said, "That's pretty much what I was going to say, ask Bailey for more help. Maybe if he could get out of here and use a phone, he could call the paper and find out who the source was. You know, just check it out."

Tracie shook her head frowning, "That might work if it hadn't been three years ago and if Bailey ever left this place, usually he has someone else bring him his groceries and things." Sensing the disappointment growing in Max she continued. "But maybe he can get us a bit more information, who knows. You never know, unless you try, right?"

Max shrugged. The hope slowly faded. "Yeah, maybe he can get something more."

Deeply uneasy, Tracie glanced at her watch. "It's nearly one a.m. We can't go there now. We can get word to him tomorrow and ask if he can get any more articles on the two of you."

"I suppose we could sneak out on our own and find a phone." Max suggested dolefully. The idea sounded so ridiculous that Sam and Tracie ignored him.

Tracie sat up quickly as though she had leaned on a tack. "You know, Max, if Ben went looking for you and they said you were missing, he may not know where you are either. I mean, he could be out there somewhere right now looking for you." They all nodded in agreement a grin played on the corners of Max's mouth; he might be getting closer to his Gramps after all. His emotions suddenly felt like a yoyo.

Nearly an hour later, with all the papers painstakingly gone through, the three decided they had better get to bed; daybreak would arrive soon. Stretching and yawning, they gathered up the pile of papers that had been much smaller and neater before they had torn through them. Quietly they blew out the remaining speck of candle and exited the library. On the alert they entered the hall and snuck back through the chilling old place to their rooms.

Remarkable Bird

CHAPTER SEVEN

Monday's dawn brought with it cold winds and a black, threatening sky. The wind howled so loudly Max was sure the roof would end up in another zip code if it continued. That of course might be ok, he thought, maybe they would be forced to shut the school for good. "Hmm, now that would be just too bad," Max muttered sarcastically to himself as he lay bundled in his small worn blanket. He would have been content to roll over and go back to sleep rather than leave his bed and step onto the cold, damp floor. However unknown to Max, today was to turn out to be a very exciting day.

Max stretched and yawned he could see steam roll out his mouth with each breath; he gawked at the screen of cobwebs as they swayed in the breeze that entered through the cracks in the walls.

Sam had slipped out the door earlier to clean up for class, apparently so had Gorfus and Rubin. Max looked around and observed that Lenny was just standing there sneering at him. He evidently didn't want to start anything while his buddies were out.

He acted as though he wanted to say something, but lacked the nerve to confront Max when they were alone. Max dressed and prepared for school in cold silence—almost more unbearable than the harassing digs he'd grown used to.

The silence was broken when Rubin burst through the door, his wide mouth and large nose twisted in a mock grimace. Rubin was the quietest of the three, yet he treasured any chance to make a face or laugh entirely too loud at cruel pranks. Rubin's arrival was exactly what Lenny needed to pump up his ego. Lenny grabbed his school books, taunting Max, "You better stop messing around, or you'll be late for class you stinking maggot. Just think, you'll be stuck in a room cleaning up dung or something equally gross, like the toilet brush that you are."

They both laughed as they headed for the door. As Lenny opened the door to leave, he hacked up a huge, green, slimy ball of snot and spit at Max's foot. The boys headed down the hallway, laughing hysterically. "One of these days, he'll go too far," Max mumbled while changing his sock.

A moment later, Sam entered the room. "Hey, what was all the laughing about?"

Max held up his sock so Sam could see the nasty green snot sticking like glue to the top. "Whoa, that's not good. Those guys are warped! Max you are seriously going to have to stomp Lenny if you ever want any peace…" Sam shook his head.

Max threw his sock into the garbage can next to the door, found another, pulling it on with a growl. "Those three are just not good, not good at all," he grumbled. They left the room to begin the day.

This day was like all the other days: the teachers unhappy to be there, the wicked kids harassed the nice kids, meals inedible. Yes, Max would have to say things were normal, with the exception of science; it was a bit more exciting than usual.

Miss Fidget usually stood in front of the class, lecturing the students about the earth and its inhabitants, or something equally boring which made Max wish he were one of the chairs in order to avoid hearing her, or see her for that matter. She was by far the nicest teacher of all – not mean, just distant. She was short and stocky, with spiky brown hair that stuck up like porcupine quills. Her dark brown eyes were hidden by thick, black-rimmed glasses. Her petite turned-up nose seemed stressed keeping those heavy frames in place, so she constantly pushed them back up onto her face with a wrinkle of her nose and a loud sniff. Occasionally her middle finger shoved them back into place in a somewhat rude gesture. Her voice was so monotonous that even the most exciting subject could seem dull, but today she had a large black raven sitting in a cage on top of her cluttered desk. The shiny black bird looked entirely too large for the small cage; his coal black beady eyes followed everyone's movements. The students filtering into the classroom were staring and talking about him. Lenny and his goons paused to stick pencils inside the cage, trying to poke him. Miss Fidget walked in just as the three boys were about to make contact.

Miss Fidget clapped her hands together, "Boys, kindly remove those pencils from my birdcage before they end up sticking out your ears." The class roared with laughter as Lenny, Gorfus, and Rubin turned a rosy shade of pink. Surprisingly they did as they were told and pulled their pencils out of the cage and took their seats.

Miss Fidget cleared her throat to get everyone's attention. "Today, class, I have a special guest. This is a Madagascar raven. He isn't generally found around these parts, yet he's been hanging around for quite some time. I caught him so that we could study him and learn about birds."

Tracie poked Max with the eraser of her pencil and whispered, as she pointed the pencil towards the caged animal. "Max, that's the same one that watched you on the first day you came here."

"It just looks like a big black bird to me, what makes you think it's the same one?" Max asked.

"See the big notch out of its beak? I remember wondering how it must have got there. Maybe this is the same bird you saw that night with the bat."

"Wow come to think of it I think —yeah it is the same bird, I'm positive that's the same one. It's looking at me the same way it did that night." The bird stared at Max and actually winked at him.

Miss Fidget continued her lesson on feathered vertebrates. Toward the end of class, she took him out of the cage and held him so the students could see the wingspan. At that moment, the raven, affectionately named Ebb by the class, flapped his huge wings and took off above their heads. The bird flew around the class its large black wings sending currents of air throughout the room. Max watched as a small black feather drifted downward.

Miss Fidget shouted, "Oh my! Everyone be still now."

Some of the girls screamed and ducked. Others just watched in amazement as Ebb swooped around the room and finally perched atop a bookcase. Miss Fidget held out bits of grain trying to entice him closer. Ignoring her, Ebb shot into the air and flew low over Lenny, Rubin, and Gorfus's desks. Plop, plop, plop. He deposited three wet, sticky piles of bird poop on their papers, and then came to rest back on top of his cage.

Even Miss Fidget laughed, "Well then, students, do we all see why you don't poke pencils at our lovely feathered friends?" Laughter rang out again at the expense of the three.

The lecture had been the best yet, Miss Fidget's voice had an air of excitement as she announced all of the do's and don'ts of ravens. She had even gone so far as to let each student touch Ebb. Lenny, Rubin and Gorfus of course declined; they sat with arms folded across their chests, drab expressions pasted on their faces. Most all of the other students had been entranced by her presentation.

When class ended and the other kids were leaving, Max, Tracie, and Sam lingered in order to take a closer look at this mysterious animal. They stood in front of the cage, admiring his beauty. Miss Fidget told Sam and Tracie how she'd managed to catch him while Max stared at him warily.

"I'm not a bird, you know."

Max looked around at his friends and the teacher, who were still talking. He looked back at Ebb and stooped lower, "You're not a bird?"

"No, I'm not."

"What are you then, if you're not a —?" Max suddenly realized he was actually having a conversation with a bird or whatever it was. He looked around to see that his friends and teacher were still talking and had not noticed Max and Ebb.

"Why do you say you're not a bird? How can I hear you talk?" Max looked under the table to see if someone was underneath talking for him. "Um, there's no one under there," Max said out loud. Realizing he was being watched, Max moved away.

"Having a good conversation?" Tracie asked amused as she walked up next to him.

"Did you hear him talk to me?" Max whispered to her.

She looked somber, "No, but we heard you talking to him."

Max felt his face heat up from his neck to his eyebrows. For Miss Fidget's sake he fibbed. "Yeah, well I thought maybe I could get him to talk back." Clenching his fists Max left the room in a bit of a huff, while Sam and Tracie had to jog to keep up with him.

"Max, stop will you please, wait for us!" Tracie said breathlessly as they caught up with him.

At the end of the hallway Max stopped and said, "Well, it happened again. The bird DID talk to me and it understood what I said. It said it wasn't really a bird. Its beak moved. Unlike the bat, it actually talked."

Sam and Tracie looked to each other then back at Max. "There is something strange about the fact that he has followed you around for years. You don't even know how many times he may have been around—you just didn't notice him until now." Tracie smiled. "For your information, we do believe you, Max."

"I can't imagine what's next." Sam said as they hurried to class.

The rest of the day seemed brighter after the incident with the raven. As long as someone believed that he wasn't going nuts Max was satisfied, and his two best friends were, without a doubt on his side—his side of what he had no idea.

The remainder of that day Max smiled every time he saw Lenny and his friends, remembering Ebbs sweet revenge and the mess he had made on their papers. One thing for sure: they'd been embarrassed enough that they were almost civilized the rest of the day.

Classes seemed to move quickly; excitement was in the air, because the holiday weekend was coming up—giving the kids five full days with no schoolwork. They couldn't leave the grounds, but it was nice having their own time. Assignments handed out at the end of the day mounted, so the students would be kept busy at least the first two days of break. The few staff who stayed on the grounds didn't want to be bothered by students, so they wanted to keep them as busy as possible.

After class, Max, Sam, and Tracie set to work catching up on as much homework as possible so they'd have time later to investigate Bailey's information. Sitting around a table in the activity room, the three friends studied compulsively for nearly three hours. It was Max who finally broke the silence with a loud yawn and a sigh. "What if we lock those three in a room for the morning of Christmas so they can't get to the food and gifts?"

Tracie smiled. "Yeah, I can just hear Mrs. Rosenblam saying, Max, you're sentenced to scrub the floors for the rest of the vacation for being so mean to my little pet, Lenny.'"

"With your toothbrush, Mister Morgan—and begin now," Sam finished. They laughed as they thought how much that sounded like something Mrs. Rosenblam would say.

"Well, we could sneak up on them, whack them over the heads then blind fold and tie them up. Locking them in one of the deserted rooms would be no problem then. No one would know it was us if they didn't see us." Max was smiling and his eyes were staring off as though he was having a very happy dream.

"Sounds good, but we'd get blamed no matter what." Sam groaned as he continued. "No, I think we'll just have to follow them around. If they start looking for things to get into we should be able to catch them at their own game." He watched the wishful appearance leave Max's face.

"That could work, you know. There are three of us and three of them. We can each keep an eye on one of them; if we notice things getting out of hand we can let out a yell and alert someone." Tracie said.

"I still think it would be fun to just lock them up for a day. Can you imagine how nice a day that would be?" Max said.

"Yeah, that would be nice," they agreed.

The dark shadow belonging to Rubin slipped away from the spot where he had crouched. He had just listened carefully to Max's conversation. His one objective was to tell Lenny what he had overheard. He raced up the steps two at a time. "Really well I'd like to see them try and lock us up, or even follow us"—Lennys voice trailed off. "Unless we made sure they followed us and then we could get word to Mrs. Rosenblam. You know we could have a perfectly great holiday without those sniveling little cowards. They would get into so much trouble if we made it look as though they stole the food, gifts, and" he laughed to himself "that stupid bird. It's perfect. I tell you this is what we have to do." Unknown to Max and his friends a plan to discredit them was in progress.

The evening ended early, but not before they stopped in at Bailey's and asked if he'd found more articles for them. He hadn't, but they were to check back at the start of the school break. That night all three turned in early.

The last day before break dawned cold and white. A new blanket of snow beckoned the students out to play. The staff seldom let the kids out, let alone in the snow or rain, as they didn't want to mop the floors. Max stopped at the front door and peeked out the window, he stared at the dark black clouds hanging low over head. Wishing he could go sledding or have a snowball fight was futile. "Oh, how fun it would be to chuck one giant snowball at Lenny," he mumbled. Turning away forlornly from the fresh white day he headed for class.

The first class that morning was full of laughter and noise. The students were excited about getting a break; therefore the day went by slowly. The teachers didn't seem nearly as happy as the students—but of course that was normal. Max barely paid attention to the lessons, as he had been wishing all morning long that he had somewhere to go for vacation. Class after class, the hours trudged by, and the snow outside grew deeper and looked more and more inviting. As Max stood looking out the window before the evening meal, Tracie joined him.

"It would be fun to throw a snowball or two, wouldn't it?" She asked him softly. Max nodded looking up at the gray sky watching the white flakes soaring downward.

"Yeah, even just running through it would be fun."

Sam walked up behind them and with a growl in his voice reminded them of what they all knew. "Well, just forget it. The wardens won't let us."

"Maybe later we can sneak out." Max laughed at his own silly thought. They reluctantly left the pristine sight and headed to chaos within the walls of the cafeteria.

Dinner that evening consisted of leftover spinach, liver, cabbage, dried bread and beans, all mixed together and poured over a lump of mush. By the time they finished choking that down, they were drained and ready to get a good night's rest. The teachers, however, had other plans.

"Attention, students!" Mrs. Grimley, the head of activities, stood before them, her crooked nose and pointy face belched out an almost froglike tone. "Tonight is the night before your break starts, and this cafeteria is a mess. It is your responsibility to completely clean and disinfect everything in this room. Do you all understand this will be done before you go to your rooms?"

Mrs. Grimley was not as mean as some of the others. She just came up with some really awful ideas. As activity director she stunk. She was supposed to find activities, not lousy jobs the kids could do for the staff. Just once, it would be nice if she said, "OK, CHILDREN, GO MAKE A SNOWMAN AND HAVE FUN." A loud murmur of moans and groans echoed the room.

"Wouldn't you think that would be their jobs, not ours?" Tracie complained.

The students didn't move. They were all still complaining to each other as Mrs. Rosenblam strode into the room shouting at them with her meanest voice while slapping a wooden yard stick on the corner of the table. "Students while you are all sitting there complaining, this room is certainly NOT cleaning itself, so GET BUSY NOW." The students all but fell over themselves as they got to their feet and began a disorganized attempt at cleaning up. The noise and disarray swarmed the room for hours, when finally, miraculously, the room had been thoroughly, yet confusingly, cleaned.

Several hours later Mrs. Rosenblam stepped into the room. She stood before them with a rather appreciative look on her face, her long neck twisted around looking over the entire room. Max half expected the head perched on her shoulders to do a full circle. "Well then, you are all free now to enjoy your vacation. I do, however, expect everyone to behave and to get all of their school work done before you lay around the next five days."

A Decent Meal

CHAPTER EIGHT:

The students left the cafeteria, trying to move slowly despite the urge to run; they knew Mrs. Rosenblam would call them back if for one minute she didn't like the way they left. Some students went to their rooms, since the hour was late and the building cold, others went to the library to get a head start on their homework so they could get it out of the way. For the first time in years the library could actually be used, thanks to Max—or whatever had cleaned and organized it.

Max and Sam stood to leave the cafeteria. The boys and Tracie had waited until everyone else left so they could discuss when to meet with Bailey. As they turned to exit the cafeteria they saw Lenny, Rubin, and Gorfus hurrying past them, whispering and talking; they appeared to be carrying something. "Did they see us?" Lenny asked Rubin. Rubin nodded as they hurried ahead making sure they were followed.

"Hey did you see that?" Tracie whispered, pointing out Lenny as he rounded the corner looking as though he were more then a little proud of himself. "I think they might be up to something," Tracie added.

She looked up at Max who smiled and said, "Yeah, let's follow them."

They trailed far enough behind so they wouldn't be noticed, using open doorways and trash cans for cover. The three boys led them down the hallway and through the kitchen. Along the outside kitchen wall, the boys pulled a cabinet away from the wall, looked around, and stepped behind it. Max grimaced and looked at Sam and Tracie.

"What the...... did you two hear that, it sounds like one of them is singing a song." Max tried to make out the words. "It's coming from them alright but it's not any of their voices, it's a strange humming sound." Max frowned.

"I can't hear anything but them laughing and whispering. I don't hear humming," Tracie whispered.

"Let's find out," Sam motioned them forward.

Behind the cabinet they discovered a long, narrow, stairway leading down into the bowels of the building. They slipped inside and pulled the cabinet back in place behind them. It was very dark and none of them recognized where they were.

"I never knew this was down here." Tracie said with surprise in her voice.

Sam held his finger up to his lips in a shushing gesture as they tiptoed down the steep flight of stairs.

Across the room in a lit corner, the three boys hovered around something. Sam, Tracie, and Max slid behind a stack of moldering books, straining to see what the boys were up to. Lenny pulled back a blanket and said, "Okay, now let's pull all its feathers out, that'll teach this stupid bird to make a laughingstock of us—hurry so we can leave those three to get caught with the featherless bird."

"We should pluck its feathers out, and then put it outside in the cold." Rubin whispered.

"No we have to leave it here so the three pansies get caught with it. Have they followed us down here yet?" Lenny asked looking around.

"I don't think so." Gorfus said straining his eyes in the darkness he scanned around the room noticing no one.

Max looked around the pile of junk, he could see now where the humming had come from, it was Ebb; they had somehow stolen him from Miss Fidget's class room.

Sam started forward to rescue Ebb, but Max grabbed him and whispered, "Hold it. I heard the bird say he'd be happy to have them try and pluck his feathers."

As Lenny reached inside the cage, his hand was suddenly transformed into a feather. A willowy gray feather swayed from the arm that once connected to a human hand. He pulled it out of the cage and yelped in surprise. As Lenny called for help from his friends, his face seemed to freeze in place with his mouth wide open. His two buddies watched in horror, slowly backing toward the steps. Lenny advanced on them, gesturing with his good hand, still trying to move his mouth.

The three boys charged up the steps, their eyes wide with horror, as they disappeared. Max cautiously approached the birdcage. He could hear the bird cackling with laughter.

Ebb took in Max's wide- eyed bewilderment and said "Don't worry you are the only one who can hear me. I think I just taught those three imbeciles to mind their own business."

Sam and Tracie stepped closer and watched, as Max frowned at the bird, focusing on his inward conversation. Finally he turned to them and said, "Listen, don't ask me how, but he is talking to me as plainly as you would."

Sam held out both hands. "No problem. I'll just about believe anything after this. How did he do that with Lenny's hand and face? I hope it's permanent."

Tracie was stunned; she stood stock still managing to mutter incoherently something about, "Seeing the look on Lenny's face was worth a fortune." A short conversation continued whereas Max visibly spoke to himself since the bird's voice was silent to the onlookers. Tracie calmed herself, finally realizing this was indeed happening. Bravely, she stepped up to where Max and the bird visited amiably.

"What are we going to do with you Ebb?" Tracie asked, looking down at the big black bird actually expecting an answer.

Ebb waggled his tail feathers, answering with a mischievous snigger. "Give me a big ear of corn to eat and turn on some music."

"What did he say?" Tracie asked.

"He asked for food and music," Max stated.

Sam looked puzzled, "Why can't we hear him when he talks? What is it that makes you able to hear him and we can't?"

"Heck if I know. Why are all of these other strange things happening to me?" Max peered into the black, beady eyes; he felt a kind of safe, comfortable feeling for the first time in a long while. "Ebb, can you tell me what's going on around here? Why I can hear you? How Lenny's hand turned into a feather?"

Ebb fluffed his shiny black feathers and stretched his wings one at a time. "Listen kid, I'd like to fill ya in on all this, but that just ain't my job, ya know. I'm here to keep an eye on you and sound off if there are any problems."

"Have you been around the whole time I've been here? Who sent you to watch me? Are you the same bird that flew past me in the hall that night? And what do you know about the green-eyed bat?"

With a loud sigh, Ebb said, "Well, kid, it's like this: I came here from the start just to watch over you. We watch you very closely one way or another, whether we are physically here or not. Who sent me is another story. It's very long and confusing; at least it would be for you right now, so let's just leave it at that. I simply cannot reveal much more to you—oh," He added hastily. "The bat's name is Dramid and his job is the same as mine—to keep an eye on you and to protect you."

"I don't get it; protect me from what or whom?"

"Can't tell ya that either. Sorry, kid. You just need to know we will be here to help when we can, okay?"

Tracie spoke up. "We need to take Ebb back to the science room, before they miss him and we get caught with him. Sorry Ebb I wish we could set you free but of course you can probably set yourself free."

The bird squawked at her, and then spoke to Max. "No need to worry about me. I can take care of myself. In fact, I think since we are all here and it's nice and quiet, why not have ourselves a bite to eat?"

"How can we have something to eat? We have no food; we need to get out of here. We are going to be in all kinds of trouble when Lenny tells the teachers about his arm and how it happened in the basement, they'll come down to check it out, and we'll be caught down here."

"Oh that? Well, ya see, by the time they got up the steps they were back to normal and their memories about the whole episode erased. Served those three hoodlums right. They're nothing but trouble."

Max relayed his conversation he had just had with Ebb to his curious friends; he looked around the dismal basement. "What kind of food could we find down here?"

"Not a problem. Check this out." Ebb popped out of his cage, flew across the room, and landed on an old table in one corner of the room.

Tracie's mouth dropped open. "Oh, wow, look at this!" She said as she walked over to where Ebb was perched looking very pleased with himself. Max and Sam ran to join her. The table overflowed with pastries, donuts, pizza, finger steaks, cheeseburgers, fresh fruit, and mugs of unusual looking juice of a lavender color. Max just stood there, too shocked to move.

Breaking the silence, Ebb said, "Hey, what gives? You kids gonna eat or just stare at it?"

Taking a step forward, with a strange look on his face, Max was unconvinced, "Is this for real?" He expected it all to disappear if he closed his eyes and reopened them.

"Yeah, kid, dig in." Ebb picked up a finger steak with his beak and began to rip it up. The three followed his example, stuffing their hungry stomachs as fast as they could.

"This is great, Ebb!" Sam spoke around a mouthful of chocolate éclair.

Max paused around large bites of pepperoni pizza long enough to say, "He said thanks; he's glad to hear that he made us happy. By the way, he says his name is Beuffus, but says he likes Ebb better, so let's stick with Ebb as long as he's a bird."

They nodded in agreement while they chewed in haste. The bird definitely seemed more like Ebb than Beuffus.

Max wondered what Ebb meant when he said, "As long as I'm a bird." What else could he be? When they couldn't hold another bite of food, Max and his friends reclined on a musty couch in the basement's corner.

"Thanks, Ebb, that was perfect, how did you do that?" Max questioned.

Ebb perched on one arm of the couch, near Max. "You can ask, but of course I can't tell you."

"I kind of figured you'd say that."

"Don't worry, kid, you'll find out soon enough. In the meantime, let's wrap this up so you can all have leftovers; maybe even take some to your friend Bailey."

"You know Bailey?" Max asked.

"Well of course. I told you I watch over you, that includes visits to Bailey."

"Yeah I guess you would know a lot about what I do, but I haven't seen you around that much. It must be pretty dull hanging around here watching me?"

"We're not always here, but enough to know this isn't a good place. I can't always intervene when things go wrong, but I do what I can."

"I just don't know who you're watching me for. Is it my Gramps?" Max's eyes lit up with the thought of it.

"Hey, kid, sorry but I can't tell ya anything. See, if I don't screw this one up, I'll get out of these feathers and back to my old self, so I gotta do as I'm told. You understand, don't ya? I promise you'll find out soon." Ebb's black eyes seemed tormented and Max did understand, but that didn't stop him from wanting answers.

"Just one more question then. What do you mean back to your old self? What are you really?"

Ebb blinked, looked around as though others could hear him, and said with a sigh, "No harm in telling you, I'm really a man. Let's just say I messed up something once and got turned into a bird. I can't even do many of my own spells because of the curse." He cawed in dismay. "But, if I do well with you the curse will be lifted, I can choose my own Orraguise, or for the sake of your understanding, the term would be closely related to disguise. Anyway" he continued not noticing Max's astonished look. "All my powers will be restored. You see being a bird limits a lot of one's powers, that's just the way it is. Now, no more questions for awhile, agreed?"

"Yeah sure," Max said. "I'm sorry you're a bird, but I'm glad you're watching over me."

Ebb bobbed his head up and down. "Thanks, kid. It's been entertaining. Again! What now?" Ebb groaned flapping his wings. "It's about to get more exciting in a few minutes. You'd better hide right now!"

Dragons?

CHAPTER NINE

Max glanced at Sam and Tracie, relaxing on the dusty couch. "Hey, you two! Ebb says we should hide—right now."

Tracie and Sam jumped up and slid behind the sofa. Max hid under the table, pulling Ebb and his cage down with him. They heard footsteps coming down the stairs and a moment later Lenny, Rubin, and Gorfus appeared.

"I thought you said they wouldn't remember anything," Max whispered.

"They can't. They're up to something else at this point. No good, I assure you." Ebb responded.

The three boys entered the basement, carrying several packages and a heavy looking cardboard box. Lenny groaned as he set it down on the floor, then the boys looked around with self-satisfied smiles.

Max craned his neck trying to hear the muffled conversation but he was too far away to catch all of what was said.

"Now we'll have some fun" Lenny said.

Gorfus glanced at the watch on his wrist. "I told Mrs. Rosenblam that I overheard Max and Sam discussing that they would meet downstairs at ten tonight, which is not long from now so we better hurry.

Lenny looked up at the steps, "I hope Max and his pals get here before she does."

Rubin smiled, "They will. I left a note in our room telling them to go to the cupboard in the kitchen and pull it back and go downstairs, I signed my name as Arabeth. The note also said that she found something out about you and she wants to tell them about it, they'll come."

They sat on the floor around the boxes and began pulling out gifts wrapped in news paper and food—evidently what had been prepared for Christmas dinner. With horror, Max recognized the prized cigar box he'd received from Gramps on his birthday.

Before he could rush out, Ebb cautioned him. "Just wait and see, Max. They won't get the box to open. Trust me."

Lenny pried at the lid, but it didn't budge. Grunting, biting his bottom lip, he fumbled with the tiny latch. At the split second Max thought the box wouldn't resist Lenny's assault, there came a loud pop and a flash of light. Lenny flung the box away with a loud yelp like a wounded dog.

"What the heck?" Rubin jumped up and walked over to the box, circling it warily as though it were a snake about to strike. Lenny lay on the floor nearby, moaning and holding his burned hand.

Max held in a chuckle and asked Ebb, "How did you do that?"

"I didn't. It's a spell put on the heritage box. No one but its intended owner or someone with a pure heart can open such a box depending on the spell of course."

"A- WHAT? What exactly are you talking about? Curses, and spells. Your talking some far-fetched ideas— that are all— like magic and —. Exactly were do you come from. And, who would put a spell on my birthday gift? It's a bunch of silly stuff my Gramps gave me years ago."

"It's not silly at all, kid. This gets kind of touchy now, so don't ask anymore questions. We've gotta get those three dolts out of here."

A loud crash and a light coming on from the top of the steps sent Lenny, Rubin, and Gorfus into hiding. They scattered, behind a pile of junk under the stairs.

Max slid out from under the table as Tracie and Sam stepped out from behind the couch to see what was going on. Before they had time to realize what was going on, Mrs. Rosenblam, Mr. Crater, and Mrs. Belfie appeared before them at the bottom of the stairs.

Mrs. Rosenblam bent and started rummaging through the bags and boxes strewn across the floor while Mrs. Belfie cradled the large pale turkey in her arms as though it were an infant. Mrs. Rosenblam gave a piercing look in the direction of Max and his friends. "Well well, we caught our little rats in the act of stealing school property and other students' property." Mrs. Belfie scowled as though she where about to cry. Her shriek echoed the walls "They also took all of our food for Christmas dinner, now we know who has been doing that for all these years."

Mrs. Belfie shrieked as she peered into the large box that Lenny had lugged down the stairs. It contained the stuffing, sweet potatoes and the other foods for their dinner.

Mrs. Belfie was a short, squat woman, she spent her days grumbling about this and that while she tottered around the kitchen. Mr. Crater stepped forward and in a loud gruff voice stated forcefully, "It seems you three have a real knack for getting into trouble."

Max pointed to the junk pile that effectively hid the real culprits and took a great shuddering breath. "It wasn't us. We didn't bring that stuff down here. It was Lenny, Rubin, and Gorfus. We saw them, they're hiding over there." He pointed again to the darkened staircase. Everyone turned and looked in that direction then back at Max. "Well now if they were actually here I think we would see them don't you Mr. Morgan, or are they invisible?" Mr. Crater said menacingly between clenched teeth.

Mrs. Rosenblam stood up from her inspection of the items on the floor and lunged forward violently shoving Max towards the back of the room. Max stumbled forward, than stopped and planted his feet to the floor with the intention on standing his ground. He was suddenly uprooted as she grabbed a handful of brown hair in her claw- like hand and dragged him along.

Mr. Crater strode up to them and grabbed Sam and Tracie by the scruff of the neck and pulled them along with Mrs. Rosenblam and Max. She looked down at Max as she dragged him along behind her. Max's stinging scalp caused his eyes to fill with damp puddles. Mrs. Rosenblam's gurgled voice came out in gulps as she tried to catch her breath while yanking him along and yelling at them.

"It's just like you—to try and put the blame on someone else. But we know Lenny, he is NOT—a big troublemaker like the three of YOU."

"You will all be punished for this deplorable deed and for your lies." Mr. Crater shouted. "Nothing is ever your fault, now is it, Morgan? Keep moving—all three of you lying little delinquents."

The teachers continued across the room pulling and pushing their victims to the darkest corner of the room, a narrow hallway led to a heavy wooden door. Mr. Crater pulled out a set of brass keys, opened the door, and shoved the three of them into the room. Tracie fell to her hands and knees as Max and Sam desperately tried to tell their side of the story.

"This is inexcusable! The three of you will stay here for the next five days. In that time, you each will write one thousand times that you were bad and will never do anything disrespectful again. If you don't have that done and offer an apology when we open the door, I will lock the door again and very possibly throw away the key. Do I make myself clear?" Mr. Crater shouted,

Max and Sam backed up to where Tracie had landed and helped her up while Mrs. Rosenblam rummaged through the pile of bags and boxes on the floor. She produced a pad of paper and three pencils, while Mrs. Belfie produced a small jug of water. The teachers left two flashlights along with the writing materials, and then slammed the heavy door behind them. The slam of the door gave Max a sinking feeling. The room was totally dark.

"I can't believe this happened. What are we going to do now?" Tracie wailed. Her voice came in breathless gasps.

Max turned on the flashlight, the weak beam barely reached across the small room. "This is so wrong. They can't expect us to survive for five days with just this little water jug. We have to find a way out!" Max stood still, waves of shock swept over him. He was oblivious to everything else, his teeth were chattering, his hands were shaking. Sam's voice echoed the room reaching Max's frozen mind.

"Max this place must be the brick building that's attached to the back of the main school. Remember last summer, the one day we were allowed out, when we lost our paper airplane and went around back to retrieve it. This has no windows or doors, just bricks and a roof."

Sam walked around the room and shone his light onto the black ceiling. "I can't see a way out of here besides the door."

From over in the corner, Max heard a scuffling noise. "Not to worry, kid. I'm trying to make a little light for us." A flash of light came from the corner where Ebb perched on a broken chair watching them.

"Ebb, how did you get in here? I'm sure glad to see you. Can you get us out of here?" Sam and Tracie joined Max as they gathered around the bird in elated admiration.

"These people are crazy. They shouldn't treat you like this. It's high time we let the Count in on this, don't you think so, Dramid?"

"Yes, undeniably this has gone on long enough. For three years we've watched Max be dishonored and ridiculed. With his noble background, we shall not allow it any longer. I shall get word to the Count immediately."

The three looked first at each other and then in the direction of the new voice, but couldn't see anything.

"Who are you talking to, Ebb?" Max asked.

"It is I, Dramid D. Vandious, at your service, my boy." Large, flapping, paper- like wings appeared before him as the slow, steady sweeps produced a breeze of cool air in the otherwise still room. Staring into Max's face were the familiar green eyes of the large bat.

Max laughed nervously. "It's you! You're the one I've been seeing; you're the one who —?" Max thought he felt the ground sway under his feet. His breathing seemed labored. "Who's— mind I can read." He was having a hard time believing any of this.

Sam stepped up next to Max and announced. "We can hear him talk." He stared into Dramid's green eyes.

"Very good, and I can hear you also," Dramid countered mockingly.

Sam looked a bit awkward. "It's just that we can't hear Ebb, or I mean Beuffus."

"Oh, that. Well, turning him into a bird was the best idea at the time; it does keep him from being noticed by humans. And he's not known for being able to hold his tongue. Sorry Bueffus, you are a bit of a blabbermouth." He continued, "Therefore, the only ones who can hear him must have powers themselves. Communicating with birds is always difficult."

"I have no special powers and I can hear him," Max said modestly.

"Ah, my dear boy, you have no idea the depths of your powers." Dramid drawled while looking into Max's eyes as though he expected him to do something phenomenal to prove the point. "We must get you out of here."

"What about them?" Ebb motioned to Sam and Tracie.

"What about them? They're of no concern to us." Dramid stated unsympathetically.

Ebb flapped his wings, agitated. "They've been Max's friends since the beginning; they have always stuck up for him and helped him."

"You're saying we should risk our necks and theirs to take them with us? I don't think that's possible, Beuffus."

Max hollered, "Take us where? And what do you mean you can't take them? They're my only friends in the whole world. I can't leave them. I won't leave them!"

"The journey cannot be made by humans. It is dangerous to expose them. We have powers they do not." Dramid emphasized the last two words with an air of overriding authority.

Max was determined to prove his point; abruptly he spoke up without much thought of the consequences; it wasn't that difficult considering it was a very small bat he was talking to. "What powers do I have? I'm just a kid." Max snapped. "And what do you mean cannot be made by humans? What am I, a shellfish?" Max glowered.

"We will reveal that later; it's a long, incredible story." Dramid said vaguely. "Right now we must go." Dramid said with an impatient tone.

Max already decided he would go nowhere without his friends. He should have felt relief at the opportunity to leave the orphanage but instead he was uneasy. Going who knows where with a bird and a bat to meet some Count person, hah, he wouldn't go alone not without Sam and Tracie. "I won't leave Sam and Tracie; so, go on wherever it is you're going and leave us behind. We've managed to survive all this time, and we'll be just fine without you." Max stumbled off in the darkness and sat down defiantly on the floor with his arms crossed in front of him. The silence was deafening.

Finally, a long sigh broke the stillness. "Obviously you're a bit more headstrong then I assumed." Dramid acknowledged petulantly as he flew over to where Ebb sat perched on the broken chair. Several minutes elapsed as the two uttered cross words. Dramid flew back to where Max sat outwardly disinterested in the conversation that had taken place, although quite the contrary. He had tried desperately to hear the exchange. "Very well then, they can go, but you have put them in danger, not I," Dramid huffed. Max sensed he had almost gone too far; the look in Dramid's eyes was unmistakably irate.

"We can protect them if we need to," Ebb winked at Max.

"Let's stop babbling then and be off. Stand back all of you," Dramid demanded. He flung his wings over his head, while he uttered a few strange words. Unexpectedly a blinding silver blue burst of light flashed before them. Filling the room stood a massive, black dragon-like creature with familiar green eyes. Max stood rooted to the spot where he was uncomfortably pasted against the wall, due to the amount of area being utilized by the dragon. The dragon's huge nostrils flared as he spoke. "Climb aboard then, all of you, and don those black traveling capes if you will. It shall be a dreadfully frigid ride."

The three of them exchanged looks of disbelief; then grabbed the heavy black floor- length garments that had appeared as mysteriously as the dragon. They threw them over their shoulders tying the hoods snugly under their chins. Max glanced from the dragon to the dark room, shrugged his shoulders and climbed up. He straddled the dragon's long body between his wings and his slender neck. Sam climbed up next, Tracie hesitated for a fraction of a second then she too followed. Tracie couldn't help but wonder if climbing up on that dragon was maybe a very big mistake.

The dragon's skin felt smooth, the great mounds of scales down the middle of his back were rough, yet pliable; still his back was warm and very comfortable. They melted into the great beast's warmth.

"Splendid, then!" Ebb squawked. "Let's be off!"

"Everyone ready then?" Hang on you three, and Max, try and get some rest—you'll need it." The three speechless kids grabbed at various flaps of dragon flesh and hung on with steadfast grips.

They were sent reeling back as the dragon prepared to launch. A deafening roar and a steamy hot breath lifted the roof from the crowded room and they rose through the top. Max looked down and watched the roof settle back in place behind them. He felt a rush of happiness; the frigid air catching his breath in his throat. He pulled the cape tighter around him as did his befuddled friends. He had no idea where they were going, but it had to be better than the orphanage— he hoped.

The night was dark, cold, and icy. When they were high in the sky all Max could see was the glistening cover of the snow which lay like a blanket over the dingy building. A shiver ran up Max's spine as he settled against the large finlike mounds for warmth. Max looked back at his two friends who seemed to be temporarily stunned; they stared back at him with dazed expressions.

They all settled back to enjoy the ride, watching as the haze drifted and faint lights below came and went as they passed above cities and towns.

Along with the borrowed capes and the heat radiating from the dragon's fins, the passengers were provided ample warmth for comfort, their exposed faces, numb and red, smiled in the dark. Ebb huddled in silence under a large flap behind the dragon's neck.

Into the evening they flew, far above the world, not knowing where or what they were heading for, but hoping it would be something better. It was an eerie feeling to be gliding along through the dark night, with not a sound other than the dragon's slow steady sweep of his wings and deep breaths. It had been a busy day; Max sat back and closed his eyes drifting off into one of the most peaceful rests he'd had in a long time.

The New World

CHAPTER TEN

As the flight through the cold dark night aboard a dragon continued, night gave way to dawn. The cold, slate colored sky turned to cobalt and the air felt slightly warmer. Below them lay a magnificent valley with lakes and frozen waterfalls; hints of ice crystals around the edges of the lake glistened in the brilliant sunshine.

The sun had been missing from Max's life for a long time; he could only remember a couple of fleeting moments when the sun shone at the orphanage, almost as if by accident. The ugly old building seemed to attract a dark cloud that surrounded it in drabness.

Max's senses stirred as he sniffed the frigid air and felt warmth on his face. A cluster of dormant trees surrounded a field of brown grass. Suspended from the trees were thousands of bats, of many sizes, their colors ranging from silver white to shining black, they occupied nearly every available branch. Max pointed out the bat-laden trees to Sam. "I've seen apple trees but never bat trees." Sam chuckled amused with himself. Max grinned deeply, his chapped cheeks painfully aching. His mood was euphoric due in part to the adventure they had just experienced, while the thrill of things to come was particularly exhilarating.

Sam tapped Max on the shoulder. "This is so inconceivable is it possible we're dreaming all of this?"

"We're all having the same dream." Max said into the air so it carried back to Sam and Tracie.

"Don't wake me up!" Tracie shouted from behind Sam.

Max hoped they would land in the spot below. Even full of bats it was the most inviting place he'd seen in along time.

As though reading his mind, Dramid shouted, "Hang on tight everyone, we're about to land."

They clutched at various handholds; the wind nearly took their breath away as they descended into the valley and made a perfect landing on the broad open field. Their legs felt like rubber as they dismounted stepping onto the brown earth.

The chatter from the bats in the surrounding trees was noisy.

"Where are we?" Max had to yell to hear himself.

"We're in the village of Transfellula, home of the Vamparian people," Ebb replied stretching his wings.

"What people would that be?" Max mumbled to himself relaying to his friends what Ebb had just said.

"No one would believe this in a million years, would they?" Sam smiled.

"And that ride, wow! What a clever mode of transportation. I do believe I'm losing my mind!" Tracie exclaimed.

As they stretched and yawned, they watched Dramid appear before them through a thick haze. The large dragon, had now taken the form of a tall, dark-haired man of slender build; the green eyes appeared colder and more callous but still unmistakable in all forms. His mustache and goatee were well groomed and he wore a long black cape. Although very striking, his appearance would've seemed sinister, if they hadn't just spent the night traveling securely with him.

"Well then, Max. May I present to you—myself the true form of Dramid D. Vandious in the flesh, and I am at your service now and in the future." He held out a large hand and firmly shook Max's hand with the slight tip of his dark head. Max looked up into Dramid's dark green eyes. The feeling of trust filled him with the confidence he needed to continue this mysterious journey.

"Okay, okay. Enough of the formalities, I would like to get out of these itching feathers as soon as possible, so let's go," Ebb squawked ruffling his feathers. Max and Dramid smiled at Ebb's reference to his feathers, and at the scruffy windswept look that he now gave them. Max relayed Ebb's statement to his inquiring friends. They all looked at the large puffed up bird and laughed at his obvious discontent.

Dramid patted his shoulder as an invitation for Ebb to climb aboard. In a disapproving voice he scolded. "I do not think I'd be so eager if I were you, Beuffus. The presence of our guests will not please the Count at all."

"We had no choice; I tell you, they've been treated horribly."

The walk across the field made Max ache for all he'd been missing: the swaying brown grass and the warmth of the sunshine on his face; these combined with the giddy feeling of adventure. At the end of the field, far in the distance, a clearing came into view. Inside the clearing sat the most massive building he'd seen—like a castle from his geography book. It was surrounded by forest and a wide river. Across the water appeared to be a drawbridge that lay open over its slow moving depths. As they drew nearer, the enormous bridge dwarfed the five travelers.

Unexpectedly they were over taken by several short stocky people whose heads appeared far too small for their bodies. They came trotting out of the trees and surrounded them. In their hands they carried primitive weapons. Their shrill voices all chimed in at once, sending a protest through Max's ears. One little man in particular stood in front of Dramid and pulled at the edge of his cape in an effort to get his attention. His slim nose flared as he talked and his hands and body never stopped gesturing.

"Hello, hello. It is nice to see you again Mr. Beuffus, Mr. Dramid. What do you have here? Oh my, they are very thin people aren't they? How was your flight? We saw you landing. I do hope it was an extremely pleasant trip. Where was it that you came from?"

Dramid stooped down in order to look him in the eye. "Well now, all of that in one breathe? I think you've said quite a mouthful. Believe me Pastry, our story is a long, boring one. I am sure you have better things to do right now then to listen to my tiresome stories. Besides, just last week I spent an extensive amount of time visiting with you and your family. Regrettably for now I must go—," Dramid nodded towards Max. "And get these thin people a bite to eat, don't you think." Dramid winked with an amused grin.

The little man's head bobbed up and down. "Oh, well of course. Yes, yes. I do think so; good bye then, for now, Mr. Dramid, Mr. Beuffus, and thin people." The clan of them trotted off babbling busily.

"How could you have visited with that man's family last week if you have been at the orphanage?" Max looked up at Dramid with a confused look.

"We said we watch over you all the time; there are many ways to do that with- out our actually being there." Dramid looked at Max with a wink and said, "It can be done. We do not spend every minute at the orphanage; there is much to be done here also." Max nodded and then changed the subject.

"What was that man?" Max quizzed.

"You mean who was that man?" Dramid countered.

"Uh- yeah, who?" Max said a little embarrassed at his referral of the smaller man.

"His name is Pastry. He and all of his family have lived in these woods surrounding the castle for many years. They tend to the very large gardens; they really are quite valuable to us."

Tracie grinned and waved at the small people who were still waving good bye to them from a distance. She looked up at Dramid skeptically "Did you say his name was Pastry? That's a very odd name."

Dramid motioned them forward and continued his story. "Yes, well you see, they were actually nameless when they were first discovered. After they started hanging around here, we decided they needed names in order for us to have conversations. As you can tell, they all like to talk at once. They chose their own names; naming themselves after their favorite foods. It was really quite humorous for a while when they told us their names. I believe there are thirty or so of them ranging from Artichoke to Rump Roast. You might have time to meet them all later." Tracie giggled while Max shrugged, his mind fixed on the colossal building ahead in the distance.

They slowed their walk at the waters edge. Max and Sam stopped, mouths open in awe, while Tracie watched the waters below ripple with some form of life. As they walked across the drawbridge and looked over the edge at the gloomy water, the thought of the orphanage with its dark, eerie pond briefly came to mind. A large green creature with scales, black eyes, and red nostrils surfaced long enough to strike fear into the three young newcomers.

"What is that thing?" As Max pointed, the creature splashed them with cold, smelly water. It lifted its huge tail high in the air to slap the water again, trying to wet them once more. Dramid, knowing the creature's habits, grabbed the three and pulled them back as an even heavier cascade rained down. With a grin at the sight of the three sopping wet faces before him, Dramid waved his hand in front of them, drying them instantly with a hot, dry sweep of his arm.

"That is Locksley. He doesn't welcome strangers, and would rather harass and eat you than welcome you." Dramid spoke with an edge of amusement in his voice at seeing the youngster's alarm.

"That, that thing has a name." Tracie managed to speak, her eyes still wide.

Ebb squawked. "He's not so bad once he gets to know you!"

"Maneuver widely around him until he knows you belong here. He appreciates fresh meat far more then the frozen beasts he is normally fed," Dramid cautioned, motioning them to move forward.

As they moved along, Max kept staring at the water, hoping to catch one more glimpse of Locksley.

Passing over the bridge, they entered a dense forest, the huge wooded area smelled of pine and decaying brush. Max inhaled deeply taking in the clean freshness. Narrow trails were cut into the earth that zig- zaged here and there. Max thought how easily someone could get lost in this maze of darkness. Unfamiliar noises rumbled through the woods sending Max, Sam and Tracie closer to their escorts.

Tracie let out a loud shriek while at the same time Dramid grabbed and held the neck of the most gargantuan snake the three had ever seen. Hanging there from a tree limb, the six foot long snake, stared directly into Tracie's pale terrified face. Dramid held the snake still, allowing Tracie to step around it. After they had all safely passed Dramid released his grip, which had barely enclosed the circumference of the snake. A scarcely audible "thanks" from Tracie was all she could manage. Max and Sam exchanged an uneasy look at one another as they glimpsed even stranger creatures. Dramid however made no mention of them.

The walk through the forest seemed slow. The rustling noises came from all directions causing Tracie a great deal of panic. Her near miss with the giant snake had left her wondering if she should have stayed back at the orphanage. Frowning slightly, Max noticed the panic in Tracie's eyes. "Hey Tracie did you think that snake sort of resembled Mrs. Rosenblam." Max asked cheeringly. It took a few seconds before she responded but it seemed to ease her tension as she grinned and nodded.

Finally they had arrived at the clearing, having made it without being swallowed alive by giant snakes, or fat snarling lizards. Tracie sighed with relief.

Max marveled at the enormous castle before him. He wondered what was housed in the two massive barns to the left of the castle. His eyes scanned the surroundings in awe. He noticed several armored men located near the top of the castle in the tall towers watching their every move.

"What is this place?" Max whispered to Ebb.

"This is our home, our fortress, our playground, our gathering place—and most importantly, it's where we learn to reach our potential. Say hello to Vonbraqoul's Castle for Higher Learning, named after its founders."

They continued across the yard and finally up the three wide steps to the doors.

Max's eyes widened with wonder. "It's incredible! It's so quiet."

"Quiet you say? Just wait until we enter the front doors." Dramid gestured toward the huge wooden doors.

They stopped at the doors that groaned miserably as they swung open, and the quiet was broken by the scurry and chatter of the daily life inside. It was indeed a castle- the stone walls and floor impenetrable.

The huge foyer, dim and cool, looked like an arsenal with weapons of many types, sizes, and severity. Some hung from hooks high on the walls while others stood motionless in barrels and cases. The stuffed bodies of dead bats hung from the walls with large golden captions below them depicting the valiant efforts they achieved while alive. One in particular stood out from the others because of its brilliant green eyes, causing Max to glance in Dramids' direction. The caption beneath the life-like figure read. *Darkgrove: The famous bat of the late, great Van Tower, flew fifteen hundred miles succeeding in saving his famed master from near certain death.* Max walked down the line reading the captions; some of the bats who had given their lives for their masters now sat on the ledge—some mangled, others headless and wingless. At the end of the row of bats, a brilliant white cat sat on a wooden shelf with no caption about its demise. Max reached up to stroke the soft fur. The cat slapped his hand, sticking four needle sharp claws into it. Max recoiled and let out a yelp. The cat turned, walked off the shelf, and onto a rock ledge half way up the wall.

"I see you have met Chains," Dramid drawled from behind him. "That cat is very disagreeable, yet he does succeed in catching a great many unwanted pests."

Max frowned, wiping the blood from the back of his hand, "Yeah I thought it was stuffed."

"Actually he sits there trying hard to torment these bats; he, however, gets no notice from them."

"Chains— what a strange name," Max frowned.

Dramid nodded his head in agreement. "He showed up here dragging several large chains, looking as though he had gnawed through them to free himself. He has been here ever since with a most unpleasant attitude, considering we did take him in." Dramid stepped back while Max continued to scrutinize the surroundings.

On one side of the great hall, in an all white background there stood a mammoth dirt colored creature. Its fur was long, heavily knotted in great curling strands, its teeth protruding and sharp. It appeared as though it were perhaps a cross between a bear and a lion. The front paws had human like fingers, but the thumbs were covered in fur. The creature held a gray animal that had a rabbit's body, with a fish's head and gills. The teeth of the smaller animal were revealed showing razor sharp and black.

The three visitors traipsed around, looking at all the creatures, wondering if they actually had existed. Dramid and Ebb stood by, amused. The scene across from the door at the bottom of a large winding staircase was intriguing and spooky at the same time. Max moved closer, examining a coffin-like wooden box with the lid off. Next to the box appearing ready to defend its contents was a huge stuffed wolf with shining teeth and deep yellow eyes, Max backed up a step as the wolfs eyes appeared to follow him. Max made a wide path around the gray wolf, stepping up to the coffin to look at its contents. Sam stepped up beside him. As they both placed a foot on the platform to look inside the coffin, a hand reached out and grabbed them from behind. Startled, they jumped and turned. They were looking into Dramid's eyes. "We really must go now."

The boys turned back, wanting to look inside the coffin, yet the firm pressure on their shoulders told them they should go. With a curt nod in Ebb's direction, Dramid led them up the winding staircase. At the top, they entered a small, dimly lit room. As they all filed inside, Ebb hopped up on Dramid's shoulder and squawked. "Don't worry now; it's going to get very dark and cold for a short time."

Sure enough, the light faded to pitch black. Max felt his chest sink to his stomach as they rose into the air. The cold rushed in on them, and then they slowed as the light crept back in. Dramid reached out and opened the door. They stepped out into a dimly-lit hallway where candles sat up on ledges and flickered as they passed. Walking down the long, cool hall reminded Max of his grandpa's cellar. Cool, moist and drafty-a musty odor drifted through the air.

Max decided this was the best adventure he'd ever had. He hadn't the foggiest idea what was happening or where he was, but all the same he felt safe and happy. His friends seemed to share his enthusiasm. They rounded the corner and climbed another set of stairs; at the top of them stood a large wooden door that creaked loudly as it opened.

Totally Amazing

CHAPTER ELEVEN

Once inside the room, Max felt the warm air; a blazing fire crackled and hissed in the stone fireplace. He couldn't keep his eyes from roving over the contents of the room. In the dim light he could see long shelves that held old books and odd gadgets. The shelves were suspended against the walls by bulky chains. On one wall, long glass cases held a collection of weapons and who knows what else. Max could only identify a handful of the unusual items. Below the display cases stood a row of sturdy tables, on them glass globes of different sizes and colors shimmered with the light from the flames.

Max was speechless as he wandered the room, eyes darting first up, then from side to side, trying to take it all in. He realized things were far too complicated to fully understand exactly what he was seeing. His mouth hung in frozen enchantment as his mind raced.

In the back corner, behind two book cases stood a massive wood desk. Flickering lamps lit the figure of a man sitting there dwarfed by his surroundings. Obviously occupied, the man's glance did not waver from the assignment on his desk. A long wooden beam lined the farthest wall behind him; under it a dozen bats of various sizes hung effortlessly. Their drab coloring of brown, black, and gray was accentuated by their multicolored eyes as they watched the visitors.

Dramid motioned for Max, Sam, and Tracie to stay put while he approached the desk and its shadowy figure. In low whispers, they exchanged a few words. Ebb sat idly by, perched on the edge of a small round table. Max wandered over to the back wall, near where the men where conversing; it wasn't his intention to spy but his curiosity got the best of him. He really needed a better look at the man sitting behind the desk. Max leaned around the end of the book shelf trying in earnest to hear the exchange taking place. Unfortunately the voices were low and the conversation short. Max caught a glimpse of the man behind the desk; his black shoulder length hair was sprinkled with silver. His silver moustache and goatee were trimmed short. His age was hard to determine as wrinkles furrowed his brow and the deepening of crows feet showed at the corners of his deep black eyes.

Clearing his throat, the man at the desk looked up from the project that had his attention; his deep booming voice startled Max. "Beuffus, would you kindly fly yourself over here so that I may speak with you?"

In a flutter, Ebb or, actually, Beuffus, flew to the edge of the desk.

"Dramid tells me that bringing these children here was your idea and that you have a good reason. Is this correct?"

"Well, yes. Of course, I wouldn't jeopardize Max and his friends had I not thought it crucial to their well being. You see, they treat him very unkindly at that school; they're barbaric." The elder man at the desk leaned forward and looked directly at the dwarfed bird nervously perched before him.

"I know how they treat him. I can see it all," he spread his arms out wide. "That's one reason you two are there—to intervene if need be. However, bringing them here could have been disastrous."

Ebb looked around the room; he blinked, ruffled his feathers, and then nodded. "That's true, I apologize." He paused long enough to lower his head then added demurely. "I was hasty. But we did make it here safely, and now we can take care of him. He is old enough to know about it, and he won't have to go back to that —that place."

The older man leaned back in his chair. He held his forehead between his thumb and forefinger as if his head ached. He took a deep breath and smiled at the bird. The discussion looked silly to Max; watching a man converse with a bird. Now he knew what he looked like to his friends while he was talking with Beuffus.

"Beuffus, I know you meant well," the older man sighed. "However I'm afraid that isn't possible just yet. His life, his friends' lives, and our way of life would be destroyed if he were caught. It just won't do to have him here until he reaches his age of potential."

In a pleading voice Beuffus warily asked. "Can we tell him anything about his true identity or about his Grandfather's capture?"

"We shall discuss some of the more important parts with him, and he may stay until, let me see—" The man looked into a glass globe on his desk, "They won't be missed for five days. They may stay until then, but not a word about his grandfather's possible location from you; I will discuss that with the boy. Do I make myself clear?" He paused, raising his eyebrows, looking peeved. "Or my dear Beuffus, I shall disguise you next as a tiny brown gnat instead of a raven." He leaned back in a more relaxed state. "Oh and by the way Beuffus, I am glad to have him here with us. It's nice to see him again." The elder man looked up at Dramid who had been patiently standing by the edge of the desk. "Dramid, please bring the boy and his friends forward."

Max moved quickly away from the end of the book case. Having only heard bits and pieces of the conversation, he was even more befuddled. Dramid stepped around the cabinet and motioned for Max, Sam, and Tracie to step forward. "Max, the Count would like to meet you and your friends if you'll come this way."

They followed him, approaching the desk. The man sitting there stood up, Max realized he wasn't small at all; the desk and chair had just given him that appearance. Standing before him grinning, Max now faced the most powerful person he had ever seen; he could feel power radiating from him. His wise black eyes were reflective pools.

He was tall, with a slight stoop to his shoulders, and the creased corners of his eyes deepened, as did his smile. He held out his hand to Max. Max took the man's right hand, a feeling similar to a mild electric current raced up Max's arm. The fleeting thought of his glove and the painting at the orphanage entered his mind.

"Max, may I present to you the very soul of our lives, leader among all leaders, Count Triad Von Housing." Dramid motioned towards the older man; he bowed slightly before leaving them standing before the Count with mystified looks on their young faces.

Count Triad's smile was genuine, and warm; respect blazed in his black eyes as he held Max's small hand in both of his. The uneasy feeling of electrical sparks faded with each passing second. As the current subsided the Count released his hand with a one-sided grin, his dark eyes relayed that he was very pleased with the strength of the current. Had Max imagined the Count's ability to communicate mentally with him? Instead of being certain that he had possible powers, he felt sure it must all be a huge mistake.

"Max my boy, it's been a long time since I held your hand in mine," said the Count reminiscently. "I do believe you were an infant at the time. You've grown into a handsome young man."

Max smiled and held the Count's gaze with his own. Clearing his throat he managed in a timid voice, "Thank you, sir. I'm afraid I don't remember meeting you."

The Count chuckled. "I am not surprised; as I said, you were very young. I was even a bit younger myself, twelve years younger I believe."

"I'll be thirteen in September, sir."

"So you will. You have grown into a fine young man. For now, we'd like to show you around, explain a few things, and give you a break from that horrible place we were forced to send you. I would first of all like to meet your friends." The Count looked at Sam and Tracie with a flicker in his eye.

Stepping forward, Sam extended his hand toward the Count. "Hey how's it going?"

"Sam, you've been a good ally for our Max and I thank you for that."

"No problem, it's nice to meet you, sir. This is quite a place."

Nodding, the Count extended his hand to Tracie, "And Tracie, you've also been good to our Max, and I am grateful. We shall extend our generosity to you for the next five days in appreciation of your faithful friendship to our very own Maximillion Von Dretti Morgan."

Max and Sam exchanged a puzzled look, "Maximillion Von WHATY?" The question soared through Max's jumbled mind. He decided to go along with this madness for now; he could ask questions later. With a wink the Count chuckled and said, "You are correct in that my boy. Plenty of time for questions later, for now, let's gets you fed. I'm sure you're hungry." Max almost swallowed his tongue; the man had just read his thoughts. Max felt self-conscious; he would have to be very careful what he thought in the company of these people. He tried to keep his mind clear as he stared at the Count for what seemed like ages. He was brought back to reality by the Count's hand on his shoulder, the other hand open- palmed motioned to the door, "shall we go?"

"Huh, Oh. Yeah, I just," Max's face reddened with embarrassment at being caught staring at the great man before him. He hurried to the door. The Count swiftly pulled the door shut with an air- tight swoosh, then stepped ahead of them all, in very long strides they advanced to the passage leading to the stairway.

The group followed the Count and Dramid down the winding stone stairs. Dramid and the Count conversed in quiet tones as they walked, unfortunately Max couldn't hear what they said. Beuffus perched on Dramid's shoulder, his head bobbing up and down with each step.

As they passed some of the more interesting rooms, the Count paused to describe a bit of the castle's history, including when it was built. The contents of some of the rooms—well actually all of the rooms appeared primitive and unfamiliar. A few of the rooms were full of students working hard at their assignments. They continued down long hallways and through fascinating rooms with objects Max couldn't recognize.

Count Triad was giving a brief history on some of the items displayed on the walls. One wall in particular seemed to jump out at Max. In an age darkened glass case, a familiar stone laid next to a strip of copper, a glove, key, map, and a knife. Max's eyes widened in surprise: these were exactly the same items he'd received from Gramps on his birthday. Rooted to the spot, Max jumped as Count Triad stepped up beside him. "Do these items look familiar, Max?" He looked down at Max with a broad grin.

Max nodded, still staring at the items in the case.

"You'll learn more about some of them while you're here," the Count assured. "My Gramps gave the exact same items to me before he went away, but I left them behind at school; the teachers will probably throw them away and Gramps, well he's gone too."

"Don't worry, my boy. Your heritage box is safe in your crate at school; Dramid saw to that. Your grandfather is also safe. We know that; we just don't know where he is."

Max's face brightened. "So you know Gramps?"

"Oh, indeed I do! I have known him my whole life. He's a great man. Max's eyes brightened at the thought of learning something about his gramps.

"Soon you will learn just how important your grandfather is." The Count motioned ahead to keep up with the others, "Let us continue to the dining room." They rounded the corner and Count Triad stopped while Dramid and Beuffus said they would meet them at the dinning hall. The Count paused next to a very short door barely tall enough for Max to enter without ducking.

"I think this will be of interest to you. This room is a play room for the very young children of the community who are here for the day while their parents are either away or working. Go ahead and take a peek, the door makes it a bit difficult for me to get in, but you three should have a look around." The Count pulled open the door using the brass ring. Max ducked inside followed by Tracie and Sam, it was incredible. An enormous hollowed tree stood in the center of the room. Little children climbed in and out through hidden passageways and then slid down long twisting slides. Laughter and happy squeals filled the air. In one corner of the room children sat around in a circle playing an odd looking board game whose miniature pieces where actually alive. The pieces talked with the children and moved on their own as the stone dice were thrown. Max couldn't take his eyes off the tiny game pieces as they hopped around the board and conversed with one another including the children.

"Hey there you three, what are you doing in my room, you do not look as though you belong here. I think you must be lost." An older woman with silver hair that hung in a long braid down the middle of her back approached Max. She was a striking woman for her age with smooth skin and walnut brown eyes. She walked slowly with a slight stoop to her shoulders.

"They're with me Garlenda," the Counts voice came in from the other side of the door where he bent his tall frame and stepped through. "It is good to see you my dear, how have you been? I am terribly sorry to have shown up unannounced but we have visitors who are unfamiliar with our castle and I am showing them around." Count Triad said, his eyes smiling as he shook her extended hand warmly.

"Oh, I am very sorry Count that I came forward so harsh, but one never knows."

"No apology necessary Garlenda, may I present to you Max Morgan, Ben Morgan's grandson, and Max's friends Tracie and Sam."

"Ben Morgan's grandson! Well it is a great pleasure to meet you. Your grandfather was a—," her voice cracked and her eyes watered, "is— a fine man. Jarvous," She called out to the back of the room, "the Morgan boy is here do you wish to see him again?" A tall slender man stood up from behind an unusually long piano like instrument.

"Max Morgan, the kid from the Morgan farm? Well I'll be dipped in buttermilk. Just look at you, you're a bit skinnier then I remember but you're growing up, getting taller." His wide smile showed a row of straight white teeth, his square jaw was wide and strong as was the large hand he extended forward and clapped Max on the back.

Max's eyes fixated on the man standing there in front of him. His mind did a rewind to that night three years ago when he was taken from his home; the eyes he saw in the mirror from the back seat of the car were the exact pair of eyes he was now looking into. Max tried to speak but the intense crystal blue of the man's eyes and the sickening sweet smell that now engulfed him made the floor sway under his feet.

Max cleared his throat, "Hi I uh," Max felt his knees weaken and he started to fall but the firm pressure on his shoulder steadied him.

"Max, Max are you alright." Count Triad held onto Max and shook him gently.

"You, you look familiar, have I seen you before?" Max asked faintly.

"I was your driver Max, I drove the car the night you left the farm, I delivered you to the Orphanage. I tried to make the drive as pleasant for you as I could. I couldn't talk with you because the woman from the state was there but I sprayed some relaxant and tried to calm you with a glance in the mirror. You were a brave boy. It's great to officially meet you; my name is Jarvous Von Henshore. I am a friend of Ben's and yours if you can forgive me."

"I'll forgive you, but what is that nauseating odor?" Max asked reeling.

"It's a calming agent it helps us to relax when we breathe it. It isn't harmful or dangerous it just smells kind of repulsive; we use it to relax our patients before we perform— certain procedures. I used some that evening to help calm you. I'm afraid I spilled some on my clothes when I was mixing a new batch earlier this morning." Jarvous said, adding with a wink and a smile. "It did calm the children a bit today while I was in here repairing the music machine, kept them almost manageable."

Max nodded, his eyes were getting heavy and he began to yawn. Sam and Tracie did not seem to share the same effect as Max; they were resistant to the sedative effect.

"I think I better go for now I seem to be putting you to sleep Max." I will see you again though. Have a nice visit." Jarvous nodded to each of them and he returned to the repair job on the piano.

Max's tiredness lifted slowly and his mind began running through that night in the back seat of the car. Yes, it was those eyes, the peaceful blue eyes and the sleeping agent that helped Max through that night. But what was the connection to Jarvous, this place, and the orphanage?

"Are you okay to continue our journey Max?" Count Triad asked concerned.

"I think so but what —?" Count Triad held up his hand. "I'm afraid we have a lot more to see Max can your questions wait?"

"Yeah not a problem I'm having kind of a hard time concentrating," Max uttered.

"Okay then lets continue." Back out in the hall Max began feeling more like his old self.

Finally they arrived to the dining area where Dramid waited with the black feathered Beuffus on his shoulder. As they approached Dramid flung open the double doors to a dining hall filled with children—hundreds of them. The enticing aroma of fresh baked bread filled the air. The room was massive, long tables sat filled with students eating; some deep in conversation, while others ate with an appetite, the likes of which Max had not seen before.

He thought to himself that the food must be good, judging from the large portions that spilled over several of the plates, while others had looked as though they had been licked clean. At the end of each table roared a warm fire encased in a stone hearth. There were five rows of five; at each side of the tables long sturdy benches held eight kids per side. The back wall housed a hot fire burning under a long stone hearth; on top of the hearth was an amazing array of hot food— everything a kid could yearn for. Beside the heated hearth was a long ice box sheltered by a glass lid. Inside cold food and drinks rested on ice. Max peered in at the contents: milk, pudding, pie, and juice of many kinds. Max stood staring; his mouth agape and watering with the aroma and sight of the food and the manner by which the food appeared. Tall black haired women in flowing capes of deep mauve appeared to float through the room keeping filled both the hot and cold foods. They waved their hands over the emptying trays mysteriously replenishing them. Max wasn't sure what caused him the most amazement; he gawked at Sam and Tracie who were oblivious to the women's activities. Once the trays were full again, the women vanished through a door in the back leaving Max stunned and curious. His attention roamed the room, unlike the orphanage; these children seemed happy and well-behaved. They focused on their feast and spoke in quiet voices.

Max looked sideways up at Count Triad. Reading Max's mind, the Count whispered, "You are wondering how the women performed such a feat." Feeling questions rise in his throat, Max started to speak, but the Count patted him on the shoulder, "I shall answer some of your questions later. Now you must eat."

Dramid led them to a heavy wooden table occupied by a blond boy and a round-faced, red-headed girl who looked no older than six or seven. Smiles lit their faces as Dramid ruffled their hair, asking them, "Would you two mind sharing your table with three more hungry people?"

The girl smiled a huge grin and clapped her hands together. "We wouldn't mind. Who are they Dramid?" The girl looked inquisitively at Max, Sam and Tracie. "My name's Jill, this here is Bobby." Jill squirmed happily on the bench while Bobby kept his attention focused on his plate of food.

Stepping up to the table Max nodded towards the two sitting at the table.

"I'm Max, and this is Sam and Tracie." Max smiled while Tracie stifled a grin at the younger girl's obvious fervor.

"It's very nice to meet both of you!" Tracie smiled and held out her hand, but the two youngsters ignored it.

"Bobby and Jill, Miss Tracie has extended her hand in a friendly greeting. This is one way people welcome one another; kind of a warm hello. You take her hand like so, make sure it's a nice firm grip or it will mean very little," Dramid held his hand out. Tracie grabbed it, and they shook. Tracie giggled and offered not only her hand but a wide grin to Bobby and Jill. One at a time, they grasped her hand firmly.

"Well, then, we've learned a lesson today on meeting others." Dramid lowered his head in a slight bow and told Bobby and Jill to enjoy their lunch. He casually motioned to a short, plump, older woman dressed in a long, drab, gray cape which swept the floor as she ambled over to where Dramid waited. Dramid looked down at Max who was still speechlessly watching the scenes before him.

"One of us will return a while later, take your time, and enjoy your meal." Dramid quietly conversed with the older woman who listened and nodded continuously as he spoke. Dramid turned on his heel and strode out of the room as did the Count and Beuffus.

The larger woman approached Max. Without a word she grabbed up Max's arm and led him to the front of the room where the food lay warming. "C'mon then youngsters, we shall get ya all filled up. I heard you were here, but I had to see for myself. My goodness it is such an honor, just look at you." She stopped long enough to scrutinize him as though he was being graded on his appearance, then she continued. "I am very pleased that Dramid asked me to help you. It's just awfully nice to meet you; I knew Ben, served him a meal or two I did." She talked so fast and was in such a hurry Max did not have time to respond. "Okay, then here are the plates," her chubby hand held up the large round dinner plate thrusting it into Max's hands. "Then ya have your utensils," she pointed to a round wood bowl filled with spoons and forks. They grabbed all the necessary items as they walked down the line. She waved her hand along the hearth, "and of course ya got the goods and I mean good. Boy, yum, yum. Get what ya want and thanks for visiting. If ya need me, the name's Freada, so just holler. I better get back to work, so go on now, help yourselves." With one last look at them she grinned warmly her round cheeks plumped enormously, and then she scurried off through a doorway.

Very eager and undeniably famished, the three of them stepped up to the hearth and walked down the full length of the hot and cold foods. Almost melting at the view— mountains of mashed potatoes, rich brown gravy, piles of fried chicken, thick hunks of fresh buttered bread, spaghetti with meat sauce, macaroni with creamy yellow cheese, bowls of fresh fruit of several kinds, the apples so red Max could taste them just by looking at them. The smell of the peaches made Tracie's mouth begin to water.

The line of choices stretched nearly the width of the room. Max wondered how he could possibly make a selection; this was more food than he'd ever seen in his life. Sam and Tracie stacked their plates so high with food that they had to walk very slowly back to the table. Max really wanted a sampling of everything; however, he did not want to appear piggish. He decided on his favorite first, and if he still had room after that then maybe he'd go back for more. He chose two chicken drumsticks, a heaping spoon of mashed potatoes and gravy, and, of course, a buttery piece of the warm bread he had been drooling over since he entered the room. A purple red apple teetered on his plate as he walked back to their table; Max nodded and smiled at the other kids as he passed. One table held a group of boys who reminded him of Lenny, Rubin, and Gorfus. These boys stared at him without responding to his friendly smile. One sandy-haired boy leaned back against the wall with his arms crossed and a scowl on his face. Learning years ago to steer clear of trouble, Max made a wide path around that table.

By the time he sat down, Sam and Tracie had already half emptied their plates and returned to heap yet another generous portion on their plates. Tracie chewed ravenously, her mouth full as she tried to talk. "This is simply," crunch, slurp, "the best food I've ever eaten."

"Yeah" was all Sam managed, his head never lifted from the task of shoveling food into his full mouth.

"Do you eat like this all the time or is this a special occasion?" Max asked Bobby and Jill.

Bobby shrugged as if not the least bit interested in what they ate, "I dunno. I guess this is our biggest meal at the noon hour. Breakfast is almost as big, dinner is smaller. They're all okay I guess."

Max dove into a big bite of mashed potatoes loaded with rich creamy gravy. Not aware it would be so hot; it scorched a path all the way down. He was sure he felt it land in his empty stomach. He quickly cooled it with a swallow of the strange lavender juice. Just okay, Max thought, this kid must be dense. This was by far the best he had eaten in years. In fact he devoured it swiftly, and then rudely sprang from the table, leaving Jill with her mouth open as she was just about to tell him something. She had quietly watched him thinking he must be nearly starved to eat that fast.

Almost absentmindedly he heaped a bigger pile onto his plate. He returned to the table with an awkward smile directed towards Jill who waited patiently to continue her conversation until Max returned.

"Now as I was about to tell you," Jill began almost impatiently. "Don't mind Bobby he really doesn't care much about anything except playing, we always have delicious meals!" Jill squirmed around on the bench, her giggle made them all smile. With a wide grin on her small freckled face she watched them while they made short work of their second round of heaping portions. "You three look really hungry. Don't you have food where you came from?"

Tracie grimaced and wrinkled her nose. "We have horrible food where we came from. An orphanage, it's a dreadful place. You're lucky to be here."

Bobby looked at Tracie with sad eyes. "Our family was taken, so the Count took us in to care for us."

"Oh, I'm sorry," Tracie frowned. "Taken where?"

Jill's happy bounce and giggle quickly vanished, replaced by a more stoic appearance. "We don't know much,—just that the Count is taking care of things for us. His hope is to find our family."

"You two are related?" Tracie inquired.

"Brother and sister," Jill said.

"Sorry about your parents. I hope they find them. You know, Max's grandfather is missing too." Tracie declared.

Max glanced at Tracie and then to the two youngsters across the table. The look on their young faces was that of true compassion. Max realized, like him, they knew how it felt to have their lives ripped away and everything turned upside down. Yet they'd been much luckier, landing with the Count instead of the orphanage.

Max nodded and Sam broke the awkward silence. "Wow, this place is so wild." He stared around the vast room. Looking up above them he could see a maze of stairways leading every which direction. The crowd of kids was now starting to empty and the great room seemed bigger. The women who kept the food trays overflowing now swept their hands and the food vanished, leaving a clean empty hearth.

"OH, WOW! Look at that." Sam pointed to strange creatures pulling carts that held the remnants of the lunch rush. They used large soapy towels to clean the tables. Grudgingly they washed the tables and benches while loading the carts with empty plates and glasses. They also cleaned the spills on the floor. Their appearance was goat-like, hairless and small each of them wore long knit sweaters of various colors. They walked up right almost human like and their hands actually were human, only unmistakably they were goats.

"What are those things?" Sam continued to stare at the animals. They seemed aware that they were the object of speculation because they all looked at him with a most defiant stare; in fact one stuck its tongue out at Sam.

"Those are naughty kids," Jill giggled behind her hand.

"Kids you say— as in baby goats?" Tracie frowned.

"Oh no. They are misbehaved kids." Jill responded, "They have kitchen duty, I think its Jimmy, Piper, and Kate, but it is rather hard to tell. There have been quite a few that have had this duty. It depends on how bad they were as to how long they have to work and, well, remain in that state of appearance."

Max turned and straddled the bench, staring at the kids, or goats, or whatever they were.

"How do they become goats? Do they just turn into them when they are bad?" Max asked as though he didn't believe a word of it. Jill looked at Max in wide eyed exasperation.

"No silly, they have to go see Miss Hickly. She takes care of the punishments around here." She leaned closer to Max from across the table and whispered. "We always try to be especially nice to her; you see some kids get even worse. We don't even like to talk about it. I hope you three never find out how bad it can be." Jill furrowed her eyebrows and shook her small head.

Max, Sam and Tracie exchanged looks of skepticism which they shrugged off as the ramblings of over- imaginative young children. In fact for the next half hour they were entertained by many unbelievable stories that the two youngsters produced. Whether they believed them or not they weren't sure.

Max looked around the room and realized they were the only kids left in the room. Even the cleaning crew had finished and left. "They told us they would be back to get us, do you think they forgot us?" Max asked Sam. As he spoke, a short stocky man walked in —his jovial smile lit up the room. Max watched with interest as his carefree bounce carried him across the floor. He tramped up to the table holding his index finger to his pursed lips, hushing Bobby and Jill. "Well then, anyone here recognize me?" Max looked at the tousled brown hair, the dark blue eyes and the crooked grin. This fellow's face was rounded and clean shaven with a slight flush to it.

Jill clapped her hands.

Bobby shrugged saying, "Of course we recognize you."

"Is that you, Ebb or I mean Beuffus?" Max raised his eyebrows. "How did you get them to turn you back? Did you do something good?" Beuffus raised one eyebrow and patted his chest with both hands. "Well, no, not exactly but when I'm here in our world, I'm allowed to be myself. It's just when I go out on assignment that they changed me into that blasted feathered bird."

"Well, it's nice to finally meet the real you—and hear your voice." Tracie patted him on the arm.

Beuffus patted her hand happily and bowed his head. "If you're finished eating, I'll show you three to your rooms."

The trek to their rooms was a great distance; they climbed a stairway at the back of the castle, and then proceeded almost to the top floor, one large step at a time. As they rose, the air felt warmer and smelled of smoke from the wood heat.

Beuffus led them to a massive room that was furnished with tables and chairs, and bookshelves that were packed tightly with odd looking books. Bulging floor pillows lay spread around the floor next to an inviting fireplace. Worn sofas faced the window overlooking the grounds. Max wasted no time looking out the window at the view from the rear of the castle. The nearby river flowed slowly beneath a thin layer of ice. Drab trees stood like stick men while the tall brown grass seemed to wave at them. Further beyond, several small neatly kept buildings dotted the countryside. In the distance was a town bustling with people. Directly below lay the murky water that sheltered the strange aquatic beast. It felt good to have a window he could actually see out of. Peering down, over the ledge of the window, Max realized how high they really were.

Absorbed by the captivating view, Max didn't hear Beuffus in the background telling them about the room. He turned from the window, looking at his friends. They grinned when they realized he had no idea what they'd just said. Max shrugged. "Sorry, I was looking out at the town. It's nice around here, better then looking at gloom." His guilty smile gave way to a wide grin.

"That's all right, kid. I was just saying that this is the study room. The students have everything they need here without going down to the classrooms to do their homework assignments."

"This is so nice. What a great place to study," Tracie exclaimed as she twirled around the room and joined Max by the window.

Max agreed, knowing exactly how she felt. The three of them wandered around the room checking it all out. Sam strangely enough meandered to the bookcase and looked at a few of the unusual titles. When Max noticed, he gawked strangely at Sam from across the room. Having noticed Max's stare, Sam shrugged his shoulders and put the book back on the shelf. "Just looking to see what kind of weird stuff they read around here."

"Yeah, sure, whatever. Max said with a glint of humor. After all, Max knew Sam was nearly allergic to books.

"It would be great to go to this school wouldn't it?" Tracie said to everyone in the room. The only response was made by Beuffus as he clapped his hands together. "I'm glad you can stay at least a few days—but for now," his voice trailed off as if another thought had entered and taken over. "If you're ready then, let's go look at the rooms where you'll sleep."

From there they were ushered across the hallway and through several doors made of heavy dark wood, oddly enough the doors lacked doorknobs. Max counted ten doors in all. Beuffus stood in front of one of them and uttered something inaudible, then pulled Max and Sam over to stand in front of him. The door slowly opened. "Come on then, this will be your room while you're here." They entered a room containing four beds covered by heavy down quilts. A wood- burning stove crackled in the center of the room. A dresser sat beside each bed, at the foot of each a large brown trunk stood open and empty.

Max walked over, picked up the pillow, and gave it a hard punch-it was an actual pillow, not a paper bag filled with torn paper. He wanted to take his shoes off and run his feet across the colorful throw rugs that lay warm and welcoming next to each bed.

Wood shutters held out the sun. Max walked over and opened the shutters. The view looked out over the front of the castle, with the dark forest of deep green trees they had walked through earlier. Max watched as the giant trees swayed in the wind.

Max stepped back and leapt into one of the small, soft chairs that encircled the area next to the window. With the sun on his face, he leaned back and closed his eyes. "This is great! Is this where the students stay?"

"Yes, but this room is empty at the moment. We have three levels; beginners stay on this level, the next up is the intermediate level, while the advanced students stay at the very top level where they engage in special training.

Beuffus turned to Tracie, "Let's get you settled young lady, these two seem happy enough." Beuffus took a sidelong look at Max lounging in the chair and Sam bouncing from one bed to the other trying to determine which one he would choose.

Tracie and Beuffus left the boys. This time he led her down a long hall to a row of light -colored doors. They stopped at the third one. "This is the girls' side," Beuffus pointed to the long row of ten or more. The room inside was completely feminine—with bright colors and lacy quilts; the stone castle was transported to a whole different dimension.

"Oh, this is terrific!" Tracie exclaimed.

"Very good then, I trust you'll all be comfortable. Each room has a small washroom attached, and you'll find everything you will need. We'll locate some clothes with capes to wear while you're here with us. You'll find them very comfortable and you will not feel so much like an outsider if you dress like the others."

Tracie threw her arms around Beuffus. "Thank you so much!"

"It's my pleasure." Beuffus patted her head. Tracie and Beuffus walked to the hall where Max and Sam were just entering after finally deciding who would get which bed.

"Uh, Beuffus how do we open the doors to our rooms—they don't have doorknobs," Max asked.

A deep voice from behind them answered in a rumbling growl. "You just stand in front of your room and the door will swing open."

Max spun around, there in front of him stood a gigantic man, at least eight feet tall, lurking in the hallway. Tracie and Sam tripped over each other backing away from him.

"Brugo, you startled our guests shame on you for scaring them!" Beuffus half frowned with a near smile, trying not to be too harsh on the big man.

Brugo held out a husky gnarled hand with crooked fingers and long yellowed claw-like fingernails. He spoke slowly. "I did not mean to scare you. I sometimes forget my manners."

Max was the first to come forward and extend his hand. The huge paw crushed his small hand as Brugo chuckled; a loud rumble emanated from deep in his throat, and his smile revealed two rows of crooked teeth. Seeing the joy in his smile, Sam and Tracie came forward and extended their hands. They shook his hand and smiled a hesitant smile. He was a very big man with a grizzly appearance and if they had met him in a dark ally, they would definitely have gone sprinting for cover.

Beuffus tried to pat the big man on the shoulder, his reach barely meeting the shoulder and falling somewhere near his broad bicep. "This is Brugo; he is in charge of the sleeping floor. He's good at his job, and fortunately for us, he wants to be here. He works hard cleaning and he directs the students to where they're supposed to be. He also keeps the peace if we have students who need it. He is normally very gentle but can be fierce and intimidating when necessary. He'll be a good friend if you need anything."

As they left, the big man waved goodbye. His hand moving side to side as his wide smile showed an intense need for a toothbrush. Beuffus placed his fingers around the back of Max and Sam's necks and steered them down the hall.

"I believe it's time we get you three acquainted with our place. I'll introduce you to Norman, and Drakon they will accompany you. Don't be alarmed—they are unlike anything that you're familiar with, but keep in mind they both adore kids and are very energetic, much more athletic than I am. They will get you through the castle proficiently."

At the top of a flight of stairs a rope hung from what seemed like midair, as there was not a ceiling in sight. The stairways seemed infinite. Pulling on the long rope produced a deep, rolling gong sound that vibrated though the great halls. Without delay, a black dragon plunged down beside Beuffus. The large creature huffed deeply as it landed. It was a fabulous animal with a huge wingspan and a scaly hide; his crested head was bulky and his eyes appeared fierce in deep ebony. The long sharp claws clinked on the stone floor as he walked closer to the four motionless observers. The driver who was perched above holding the reins slipped down off the giant black monsters back and scurried over to the three curious kids. Swiftly standing before them he was just about four feet tall, covered with thick tangled mouse colored fur. The kids stood glued to the spot, their mouths agape, eyes wide.

"Hello Norman."

"Hello, there Beuffus. How're you today? I am just fine. Who do you have today and where do I take them? Are they new here, just visiting, or what?"

Norman stared intently at the three new faces. His matted chest rose up and down as he caught his breath. Max could barely see a pair of mischievous brown eyes through all the fluff. His head wobbled from side to side and he bounced on one foot, then the other. They could hear him talk but couldn't see his mouth.

Beuffus introduced them, then added, "Norman is our transport specialist; he knows every nook and corner of the castle."

Norman nodded, saying. "I actually used to be a dust mop but a student made a tiny mistake and well—here I am."

Max couldn't help but stare cynically at the hairy person standing before him. A dust mop he said? Just when Max thought it couldn't possibly get stranger then he meets up with these two characters.

Norman let out a squealing, high-pitched laugh, clapped his hands, and wiped off a white smudge of slobber from the otherwise midnight black hide of the enormous winged creature. "This is Drakon. He of course is a dragon. Don't let his ferocious exterior scare you, he is really very likable."

Tracie unexpectedly let out a yelp. She had been alertly watching Norman, when the dragon ran it's long scaly tongue the full length of her now slobber drenched face. "Oh yuck," she sputtered, wiping away the white foamy slime.

Max couldn't control the sudden outburst. His laugh caused Tracie to flip a gooey mass over onto his arm that he shook violently trying to displace. They all joined in a loud rolling laugh.

"Well now the greetings are over I guess you understand how lovable Drakon is." Beuffus said as he handed Tracie a small piece of cloth. She continued to frantically wipe away the evidence of the Dragon kiss. Max and Sam continued their inward chuckling.

Beuffus rested his hand on Norman's shoulder, and spoke slowly. "These three kids have traveled a long way to have a look around. Please show them the main floor and the grounds if they all wish. There is NO HURRY, my friend. This is your afternoon assignment. A nice slow stroll, if you will." Beuffus looked up at the three eager kids. "Norman is so speedy, we have to remind him to slow down and take his time."

Norman nodded his understanding and motioned for the three of them to scramble up onto Drakon's black leathery hide. Tracie climbed up first to avoid being licked again and sat directly behind Norman, Sam sat behind Tracie and Max sat behind them all. Norman grabbed up the reins and gave a firm shout "Off then Drakon."

They were off in a slow but steady plod. Norman described each of the ground floor rooms they encountered. The few upper rooms that the Count and Beuffus had shown them already were out of the ordinary, Max wondered how the main floor would compare, he had a feeling it would take days to actually see them all. Occasionally they entered the bigger rooms and found they were looking at some very strange items. One room in particular had several tall glass jars positioned on long shelves. Each of them contained different types of heads that floated motionlessly in a clear liquid. Max leaned out for a closer look. As he caught a better glimpse of the contents in the jars he decided against it and changed his attention to a less gruesome item, like the small brown bat dodging here and there above them.

The huge castle reminded Max of an anthill filled with chambers and mysterious doors, the odd stairways led every which direction. He wondered how long it would take to learn his way around. Tracie and Sam talked and pointed at the passing scenery. They entered one very large room that was full of students who stood around numerous boiling black pots, the smell was unbearable. Tracie grabbed her nostrils and pinched them tightly closed. "What is that awful smell?" she asked.

"I'm not too sure but we're not sticking around to find out." Norman said.

Drakon did a quick turn about and excited the room. Outside the stinking room Max took a deep breath while Tracie smelled her shirt to see if the odor had penetrated her clothes.

A Crocowolf

CHAPTER TWELVE

Finally the full tour of the main floor was completed. It had occupied nearly two hours of their afternoon and they had enjoyed every second of it.

Drakon came to a stop at the front foyer where they'd entered earlier that day. Norman turned around and looked at the three passengers. "Well now that's most of the main floor. Would you like to take a tour of the outside?" He observed them closely in anticipation of their answer. Max and Sam exchanged enthusiastic looks. "Sure that would be great," they looked at Tracie who nodded in agreement. Norman sniggered gladly while Tracie tried hard to see his expression through all the matted hair.

Drakon moseyed to the doors where an emaciated pale man wearing a cape that was far too big for his slight build, nodded and opened the two large doors. His watery eyes rested on Max, giving him a creepy feeling. Max stared at the older man noting how deep his eyes lay within their bony sockets. His tight skin was stretched over his protruding cheek bones and was the color of chalk. He stood there expressionless and uttered not a word, just a deep clearing of his rattling throat as they passed. Max knew it was impolite to stare yet he could not help himself. The man actually looked dead, or almost anyway.

Outside the castle the sun was beginning its downward tilt low on the horizon, a deep orange shown in their eyes while the biting cold froze their skin. Having grabbed their earlier traveling cloaks, they now wrapped them a bit snugger. Warmth from the dragon helped; however, this dragon was not nearly as large or as comfortable as the one they had traveled on earlier that day.

"I suppose you three might be cold. I, however, don't get cold - lots of fur." Norman chuckled, rubbing the fur on top of his head. The climb down the three wide steps from the door was a bit tricky for the giant beast but he did well managing not to unseat his passengers. Once in the courtyard a tall hooded man stepped forward, in his hand he held a long wooden spear with a glimmering crystal tip. Around his shoulder he carried a longbow. In the quiver on his back several wooden arrows protruded. Norman greeted him with a nod, the man in the hood nodded back stiffly. Max, sitting furthest back, instinctively scooted forward as the hooded stranger also climbed aboard the very back of the dragon, and they bound forward. Norman noticed Max was looking at the man near the dragon's tail as though he were headless.

"We have to have someone with us at all times while we are out of the castle. You know, in case we get invaded."

Max sat up straight, "Who invades? What do you mean?"

"It's not my place to tell you that information if you don't already know. Sorry, but I cannot."

Max shook his head in disgust. "Yeah, we've been hearing that a lot. Everyone keeps saying they'll tell us later."

Max fell silent, enjoying the ride in the waning sunshine. Tracie and Sam were also quiet, looking around at the strange scenery. They saw giant trees with big deep holes running through them, big enough for them to all fit through. There were tall wooden posts, four feet around, with square wooden boxes balanced on top. It looked to Tracie as though tiny shining eyes were peering out at them from the boxes. Flowers that should not have been blooming this time of year were bright purple and had strange looking creatures that resembled round squishy squirrels with feathers climbing around on them, actually eating the flowers. They all watched for as long as they could before moving past the scene.

Suddenly, a black cat the size of a large dog shot out in front of them. Norman pulled hard on the reins in order to miss stepping on the cat. "Darn you Areelias," Drakon had been thrown off course by the sudden jerk and had came close to a tall evergreen hedge. Within the thick foliage a deep growl vibrated the ground. The jerk on the reins caused the dragon to become irritated and he stood there stubbornly shaking his head while Norman was trying hard to convince him to continue.

"Keep your hands and feet tucked in close and hang on. We've irritated Gruge, and she doesn't like to be bothered. We came too close to her den." Norman said breathlessly while he continued to pull on the reins and curse under his breath at the immovable dragon. "Oh blasted you spoiled old thing, you are going to get us all eaten if you don't move." A long, furry paw with jagged claws shot out from the center of the brush. Tracie let out a yelp, flinging herself backward, nearly slipping off the other side. Sam, positioned in the spot behind her, caught her by the arm just in time. Once she righted herself she let out a ragged breath. Drakon became aware of the smaller creatures attempt to grab at them; he unexpectedly turned on the creature and blew a red-orange stream of scorching fire toward the direction of Gruge. Gruge let out a pitiful whimper and drew back within her overgrown shrubbery.

"What is that thing?" Tracie called to Norman as she patted Drakon for scaring away the beast.

"She's a crocowolf, and it's almost feeding time. We'll move away a safe distance and watch as she comes out to eat."

They pulled forward next to a stone fire pit and stopped. Drakon dropped his head and munched on the dried grass. He found a fat brown moth larva and crunched it up, swallowing it down with a gulp. Tracie was still shaken from the near miss as they sat there recounting the story. A few minutes passed when a cluster of bats flew from the castle's tower, carrying a chunk of red meat which they dropped beside the bush. In less than a second, the strangest beast they'd ever seen poked its head out, and slithered over to the meat.

"Oh, my" Tracie's jaw dropped, "what in the world?" she whispered. Norman saw the dumbfounded looks on his passenger's faces. "Guess you haven't seen anything quit like Gruge. She is one of Graygole's mistaken inventions—however we found she makes an excellent guard dog, so to speak. She comes out at night, so you must always be careful if you wander outside after dark."

Max gawked at the creature. It was long and low to the ground, like a crocodile. The long arm that grabbed the hunk of meat looked like a hairy human hand with huge claws. She had yellow eyes, green scales down the middle of her back, and gray fur like a wolf's coat over the rest of her body. Her head was half wolf and half crocodile, with a crocodile-like snout. A set of vicious looking teeth ripped the meat to shreds. As she consumed it, they could hear the crunching bones being chewed into small pieces.

Norman made a sad moan as he shook his head and said calmly, "We can't tell what she eats at night; there's never enough left to identify."

"Wow!" said Sam. "Who'd you say created her? Is he a scientist or something?"

"Something similar to that I guess. Perhaps you'll meet Graygoles, our science master. He doesn't often make this type of mistake." Norman said simply.

"Let's hope not!" Max shared an abhorrent look with Sam and Tracie.

As they returned to the castle Tracie kept looking back at the bush. Max noticed she was trembling. "Are you all right?" He asked.

"Yes. But I can't stop thinking about that hideous creature. It's so creepy. When she looked at me with those yellow eyes, I felt like a scrap of food."

Sam grinned and said, "Well, I'd rather take my chances with Gruge than hang around Lenny and his creepy friends."

"Yeah, I'd rather hang with ol' Gruge than almost anyone at the orphanage," Max added.

Tracie faced forward and tried to smile. "Yes, I suppose you're right, but I know I'll have nightmares."

"Ya know, come to think of it, she kind of resembles Mr. Crater in a rugged sort of way." Sam said grinning with mischief.

Back inside the castle, they thanked Norman for the tour and watched as he ambled off in the opposite direction. Tracie smiled. "He's so darn cute. I'd love to pinch his cheeks if I knew where they were."

As they crossed the threshold to the dining room, Bobby and Jill motioned from a table. The trio filled their plates at the long hearth, and joined their new friends. Jill chitchatted happily, asking about their day, while Bobby gnawed on a chicken leg. The conversation was light, the food once again appetizing and abundant.

Tracie looked down at her waistline smiled and said, "I guess it's a good thing we can't stay here. I'd gain a hundred pounds."

"You could stand to gain a lot of weight, Miss Tracie." Beuffus came up behind them and ruffled Tracie's hair. "And how was your day?"

They told of their adventure with Gruge and how helpful Norman had been, they asked all of their questions two at a time. Wanting to learn as much as they could about everything they had seen. Beuffus held up his hands in surrender. "Hold on there! I can't answer everything at once." He straddled the bench and joined them at the table.

They talked through the meal, scarcely noticing as the other students finished eating and filed out. Beuffus told them some of the kids were headed for the library to study while others would practice a sport called Valentia.

"Can we go and watch?" Max asked.

"Of course, finish your dinner and we'll all go." Glancing at Jill and Bobby, he said, "Unfortunately you two probably need to get back to the lab. Mrs. Sovine will think you've forgotten her."

"Oh, yeah," Bobby said. "We didn't mean to explode that pot of Scarrot guts all over the lab. I think maybe we used the wrong ingredients."

"THINK is the key word. You must pay close attention when you mix any type of brew—especially the messy ones."

"That's what Mrs. Sovine said," Jill stood and waited for Bobby. "Well, good-bye then. We'll be stuck in the lab for hours, cleaning up."

Beuffus waved at them, and they hurried out the door.

"Let's get to the arena and watch the practice." Beuffus said cheerily. Tracie looked up at him and tapped him on the shoulder. "Beuffus, is this the last day of school here before Christmas break?"

"This was the last day of class, but we all celebrate Christmas day together. A couple of days after that some of the students go home for two weeks. Others stay here and goof around, or help with housekeeping chores to earn points they can redeem for coins." Max grimaced as he thought of the orphanage and how much work he did and for nothing.

"Wow, if I went to school here with as much work as I do I'd be a millionaire," Max exclaimed.

Nearing the main staircase, Beuffus said, "We'll take the express route instead of going across the grounds under the bridge. In fact, since we're running late, I'll speed it up. This should be fun for you!"

Under the staircase was a door that lifted from the bottom. It slid up when Beuffus pulled a cord, revealing a dark cave. The entryway scarcely had enough room for the four of them to stand.

Beuffus motioned them inside and then he released the cord, the door closed with a thud. They were surrounded in pitch blackness. A faint light barely distinguishable in the distance gave the impression that it was miles below where they stood. The cave felt cool and smelled damp, like a dingy basement. Beuffus reached up and lit a candle, the light flickered and revealed directly in front of them six iron carts with two short seats in each end of them. They had metal wheels and looked to Max as though they rested on a train track. The track had deep crevasses for the wheels to lock into. Beuffus stepped out onto a platform next to the front cart and held his hand out, motioning to the seat.

"Climb up here two of you and have a seat." Max and Tracie, the closest, stepped into the first car and sat on the cold hard rusty surface.

Sam stepped up to the next car and sat down. Beuffus blew out the candle and sat across from Sam. "Alright then, let's go. Just remember to grab the sides of the seat and hang on."

Max and Tracie held on with white knuckle anticipation. Max could feel his heart pound in his chest with the thrill of the unknown.

The cars rocked and clamored through a maze of tunnels, the speed increased with each curve. After a few minutes, the air on their faces grew fresher. The faint lights of an arena came into view.

They were rolling slowly down the tracks, into the open, where an impressive view of activities called out for attention. Slowly the carts came to a stop along the top of the arena where they were deposited next to a long platform that led to a series of rugged looking steps and long wood benches.

"We made it," Beuffus winked and jumped out of his seat.

Max climbed out assessing the surroundings. His legs felt shaky and his eyes watered from the cold air. He looked at Beuffus with a wide grin and said. "That was great we must be a long way from the castle. I can't see it at all."

Beuffus smiled and looked up on the horizon in the direction they had just been. "We're not too far. The arena was built in a bowl-like area, we can't see the castle over the sides. It's like a very deep hole."

Tracie straightened her clothes as she stood and stepped out of the cart, she wiped her sweating hands on her clothes, she had been anxious about the ride, "That was quite a ride. Is that how everyone gets here from the castle?" She looked around the spacious arena and thought about how long it would take for that many people to ride the cars down through the inside of the mountain that stood above them.

Beuffus laughed. "Oh no, most students walk, some ride their horses. Others who are practiced in the art of de-materizing do so, only with supervision that is." Max looked from one to the other, stopping his stare at Beuffus.

"De- mat –WHAT? What does that mean?" Max looked baffled.

"Well, it means leave one place and go to another without anyone seeing. Kind of like disappearing, you know?"

Max stared straight at Beuffus, his eyes narrowed and his face froze in a concentrated look as he asked, carefully pronouncing each word. "You mean become invisible, and show up someplace else?"

Beuffus seemed preoccupied looking for a good seat. "Yeah, something like that pretty much." He shrugged as though it was no big deal.

The three kids watched him while trying hard to understand what he just told them. Max mumbled to the two of them. "Guess it's not much stranger then anything else we have seen here."

Beuffus motioned them to a quiet section several rows behind a rowdy group of noisy spectators, mostly other students clapping, talking, and cheering the activities on the field. They noticed Beuffus and waved and called out to him. Beuffus waved back and then pointed out a series of benches with a view of the center of the arena, "here we are. Let's sit over there where we have a good view."

On the field, a group of fifteen uniformed kids formed three huddles, five in each. Fifteen horses stood patiently by with blankets matching the uniforms. The silver armor covered most of the horse's bodies but the team colors were evident. All around the field several stuffed mannequins stood propped in various locations they too were dressed in armor. Large shining golden rings that were suspended midair ran the length and width of the field. The rings were moving quickly all around the field. In the center stood three large wooden boxes, each, the same color as the uniforms.

"How does this game work?" Max asked.

Beuffus spoke up to be sure all three of them heard him. "It's a skill-building game that offers fun and entertainment while our students learn to fight the enemy. There are three different teams: the red, the purple, and the blue. Each will mount their horses and gallop around while trying to avoid getting hit in the head by those rings that swing through the field. If a ring comes close enough to knock them off their horse, they can grab it, hang on, and wait for a teammate to ride by and pick them up. The teammate takes his or her team member back to the horse, still trying to avoid the rings.

"Why the rings?" Tracie asked.

"They act like the attack bats we fight. We try to avoid them, but we can also grab hold of both legs and then they usually can't fly correctly. This of course theoretically gives our fighters time to get to each other for help. The dummies at the ends are suited with full armor. The only penetrable spot on the body is the kill spot near the center of the chest, to the left; it's the heart. That way the only way they can win is by getting proficient at hitting that vulnerable spot, the heart. The students try and spear the dummies, while still avoiding the rings. If they manage to spear one in the heart, the spear will go all the way through and make it possible to get it to the wooden boxes in the center. They ride over to their box in the center and throw him in. The team with the most dummies in their box wins. The game ends when the last man is speared." Sam watched with curiosity, a big smile filled his face, his eyes lit up. "Wow, sounds like fun—but hard. How old do you have to be to play this game?"

"These are advanced players, but there's no age limit. Beginners don't ride horses, so the rings can't reach them. They also use smaller dummies."

A large booming voice echoed the stadium announcing the names of the players.

"The game is about to begin, would anyone like some popcorn or some jelly bats?" Beuffus asked.

Max shrugged his shoulders. "Sure, sounds good to me."

"Yeah, sure me too." Sam managed.

"Yes PLEASE." Tracie looked at her two friends in feigned annoyance for their rudeness.

Beuffus held his hands in the air then produced three buckets of popcorn and three bags of multi colored candy bats. While that impressed the three kids, so did the activities on the field. They turned their attention to the arena below, happily munching on the bounty Beuffus had produced.

A loud "ohhh" echoed through the stadium as a boy from the blue team lay on the ground, not moving. His horse galloped toward the opposite corner. A team of men in white coats ran in and picked up the student on a stretcher. Moving quickly they carried the downed player through a door under the stands.

"What will happen to that boy?" Sam asked.

Beuffus shook his head and said matter of fact, "Professor Harmrock will take good care of him. There isn't much she can't fix."

Max found it hard to keep his eyes on anyone in particular, the action was constantly moving. He was entranced at the talent on the field; it was beyond what Max had imagined.

"These teams are really good." Max commented.

The action increased and became more confusing. It was hard to keep track of all of the players and horses. They ran back and forth; dodging the rings and stabbing at the dummies with long spears. Two players dangled from the rings and were swaying around the arena, waiting for someone from their own team to pick them up. One of the purple guys pulled his horse up next to his dangling teammate and dodged underneath him helping him from the ring then transported him safely to his horse that stood quietly out of the way. The player took off again, stabbing at one of the dummies.

"It would be much easier to watch if I knew someone on the teams, then I could cheer for one or the other," Tracie hollered above the noise.

"Maybe one day, you can try your hand at Valentia, Max. Your mother was one of our best players." Beuffus winced as though he had said something he shouldn't have.

Max stared at him with eyes wide. "My, my mo—mother?" Max stammered. "You knew my mother? I don't even remember her; she was gone when I was just a baby. How do you know her?"

"Oh boy, I did it again; I opened my mouth when I shouldn't have. I'm sorry. The stories we will tell you are long and a bit confusing. We must give you time to understand what it is we have to say. If you can wait a bit longer, we'll take the necessary time. For now enjoy the game." Beuffus pointed out to the action.

Max's mind reeled; he had no choice but to accept the explanation. He closed his mouth while his mind remained a pool of conjecture. He stared at the field without really seeing it, thinking about his mother. How did the people here know her? What had happened to her?

The Invasion

CHAPTER THIRTEEN

The game continued as the fans in the stands became louder and more excited. When the match neared its final hair raising minutes and the last dummy was deposited into the blue team's box. The crowd yelled and cheered throwing up their arms and jumping up and down. The announcer was so excited he jumbled the final announcement. "We have a wew ninner it's the— the I mean a new winner the blue team has just won this match by one dummy," shouted the male voice through the microphone. Max chuckled at the announcer's mishap.

"Thank you Beuffus, for the wild day it was pretty much unbelievable." Max said. The blue team was celebrating and making final laps around the field on their horses while waving to the crowd.

They all stood up from the hard benches, and stretched their backs, arms and legs, as they chatted happily about the game. It was time to join the others for the long walk back to the castle. They were enjoying the freedom to breathe fresh air and to walk outside exploring the wonders of this mysterious place. The evening air was freezing, and the sky was filled with brilliant stars lighting the way to the castle. A huge yellow moon hung in the sky surrounded by a few fluffy clouds as if nestled there sleeping.

They followed the other spectators out the back of the stadium and then stepped out onto a well-worn path. The hard ground was covered with shiny pebbles that crunched underfoot while they trudged up the hill to the castle. The walk was a lengthy one; Max had not realized how far it was to the arena since they had practically flown down. At the end of the long path they entered a dark cave lit only by the few students who held a fire in their open hands.

"Beuffus how do they do that"? Max whispered.

"Do what?" Beuffus questioned as they walked through the dark cave.

"That," Max said, pointing to a tall, dark- haired boy who appeared much older. His open palm hand held a small flickering fire.

"Oh that. They are very advanced students." Max had hoped the explanation would be a bit more enlightening; however, nothing more was affirmed.

They continued for several minutes through the dark spooky underground. Ahead of Beuffus and his guests several students joked and howled as they walked through the maze. They noticed someone running to them from the front of the line it was a young black haired girl who ran up to Beuffus and breathlessly managed to tell him what was on her mind. "Please come help, Ryan and Irving are fighting and poor Gilda got right in the middle, please help!"

Beuffus had left to the front of the line long before the girl had finished the details.

"Come on let's go see what's going on." Max and Sam raced up to the front of the line that was now packed with students hollering and cheering on there friends who were very busy trying to beat up on each other. Max watched as one of the boys in the fight was sent crashing against the stone wall and crumpled to the floor like a rag doll. Just as the other culprit was about to pound on another student Beuffus grabbed him up and held him high above his head.

The angry student kicked and shouted, "put me down or I'll." suddenly he realized that it was Beuffus who held him there.

"Or you will what?" Beuffus asked. Max could tell by the tone of his voice that Beuffus was angry. "I think this should be handled by someone other then I, you two are to go see Miss Hickly." Without another word the crumpled student on the ground and the one who was being held motionless above Beuffus's head were gone, they had vanished.

Max, Sam and Tracie exchanged disturbed glances while Beuffus hollered. "Okay it's all over, break it up and get on up to the castle." He reached down and picked up a small snarling black dog, her beady eyes watched him and her pointy nose twitched as she smelled the air. "Thank you so much." The girl snatched up the dog from Bueffus and was giving her a sound scolding. "Gilda you naughty girl what were you thinking? That you could take on those two ruffians? Now look at you, you're all dirty!"

"Well then sorry you had to witness that but these things happen, kids do what kids do, you know." Beuffus shook his head and proceeded up the cave.

Finally they reached the end of the narrow corridor where a faint light shown from inside. Everyone was filing into the castle with its maze of halls and rooms. This time they were in the extreme bottom of the castle in a place they had not yet seen. It was rather eerie. Noises coming from the closed rooms reminded Max of a sinister movie he had seen. As they walked past a lit room, the door that lay open slammed with a thud while dreadful laughter filled the narrow corridor. Moving forward down the dark hall a deep growl startled the new comers, it was followed by an ear -splitting howl which sent a tremor through Max. His legs instinctively gave a lurch propelling him closer to Beuffus's side, then bumping into him.

Max uttered a muted "Sorry."

Beuffus didn't seem to notice.

Finally to Max's relief, they climbed the stairs to the main level then up the twisting staircase to their rooms. Beuffus walked them to the student commons near their sleeping rooms. With a jolly smile,

Beuffus clapped Max on the back. "I sure hope that was fun for you all. I haven't been to a good game in a very long time so I enjoyed myself. You three sleep well and we'll see you in the morning, which isn't far off, so get some rest."

"Thanks Beuffus, for everything." Tracie grinned happily. Max and Sam grinned and nodded.

They joined a group of students around the fire in the student commons, enjoying cookies and hot cocoa while talking about the game. They got acquainted with a few of the students who were friendly and talked freely about the night. The team members were not back yet. Max was told they had a lot of gear to put away and to take care of their horses after each match. He hoped to talk to someone who played and find out more, especially after he learned his own mother had played.

Tracie yawned behind her hand and grabbed a book off the shelf. "I think I better get some sleep. I can never fall asleep quickly, so I better start now. Good night to you all." She bound off in the direction of her assigned room. Max and Sam exhausted, also bid the others a goodnight and followed her down the hall.

Tracie carried her book. She could read all night with no one to tell her to put out the light, tease her, or make rude comments.

Warm flannel pajamas lay folded on her pillow. She changed, cuddled up in the quilt and looked at the book, HOW TO CONTROL A CHIMPANT. The strange beast on the cover made

Tracie think of Gruge and her near miss this afternoon. She opted not to read the book for fear she would have horrible dreams. She blew out the lamp. "I have no idea what a Chimpant is anyway," She mumbled to herself.

Max was thrilled to have a room without anyone picking fights and watching his every move. The boy's slipped into their flannel pajamas and sat beside the window, looking out at the faint lights of the town and the lights streaming from the castle windows.

Sam heaved a huge sigh. "This is wild. I wish we could stay forever. I wonder what it would take to get them to let us; do you think it's possible?"

"No, you heard them say only five days. They said something about it being too dangerous," Max reminded him.

"We could try and change their minds, couldn't we? It wouldn't hurt to try."

Max thought for a moment.

"I'm supposed to talk with the Count tomorrow, I'll ask him—but he doesn't seem like someone who would change his mind. He seems nice enough, but all serious. You know—a reason for everything."

"Yeah, but it's worth a try." Sam said stretching his arms.

"I'm going to get some sleep. Who knows what will happen tomorrow." Max went over to the bed, pulled back the covers, and slid between the clean, crisp sheets.

"Me too, I'm whipped. I'll sleep well tonight, an actual bed and a pillow too." Sam said jumping onto the bed.

"Yeah, nice, it won't take me long to get to sleep." Max mumbled tiredly.

"Good night." Sam yawned.

"Night." Max was nearly asleep before the words left his mouth.

In his dreams, he saw his mother hanging onto a ring that pulled her through the arena. She was wearing a white gown that swayed in the breeze. He watched as she circled around, and around, her face came into view, her eyes were shut and a peaceful smile was fixed on her face. Suddenly her eyelids opened, revealing blood red pools, every bulging vessel detectable. Max tried hard to shut out the disturbing vision, he stirred as he heard his mother shout. "Help me! Please, someone help me! Won't you call my son Max? I know he can help me!"

Max sat up in a cold sweat, his breathing ragged; the dream was so real, he felt as if he could have reached out and touched her. Before now, he'd only known what she looked like from old photographs he knew nothing more about her life. The haunting vision of her eyes burned in his brain. He lay awake for a while until the warmth of the bed and exhaustion overtook him; he fell into a dreamless sleep.

Max awakened to daylight piercing his eyes. He yawned rubbed his eyes, and tucked his head under his pillow. Quietly he tried to fall back to sleep until he gradually remembered where he was. With an excited jolt he jumped up, and hurried to look out the window. The other students were outside on the grounds piling chunks of wood and brush into a heap. They laughed and worked on the task at hand, a haze of steam streaming from their mouths in the cold morning air. They all worked together to create a huge pyramid.

Sam approached and stood beside Max. "What do you suppose they're doing out there?"

" Dunno, it looks like fun! Should we go down?"

They dressed in a hurry, slipping on the attire that someone had left for them hanging on a hook next to their beds, used the toothbrushes in the bathroom, washed up, and headed out to find Tracie.

Their attempt to enter the door separating the girl's rooms from the corridor failed miserably, leaving Max with a red bump on his shinbone. They had pushed, pulled, pried, and finally Max kicked the door with the side of his foot. Then without notice, the door kicked him back. Shocked by what just happened Max stood fixed to the spot, rubbing his shin, while Sam continued the assault on the door keeping a greater distance. "What was it we were supposed to do to get in here?" Sam grunted pulling with all the force he could gather.

From behind them, Brugo said, "You can't get in that area unless you state your business, and it must be believable."

Max shrugged. "We wanted to tell our friend Tracie that we are going down to the grounds to check things out."

"And eat," Sam said rubbing his growling stomach.

Brugo nodded. "Okay then, all you have to do is stand in front of the door and say that."

Turning back to the door, Max said, "We're trying to find Tracie."

The door opened slowly. They waved a thank you to Brugo, then entered the hall outside the girls' rooms, and knocked on Tracie's door.

Tracie opened the door and stood there with a wide grin, she too had dressed in her dark pants, shirt and a long billowing cape. "Don't we look a sight?" She said. "I suppose we will fit in much better, but I feel a little awkward."

"Looks alright to me," Sam said, "at least they're clean."

"And they actually fit, I didn't have to tug on them until I was blue in the face," Max added.

Max recounted his odd dream for Sam and Tracie as they exited Tracie's room and walked down the long hall to the first set of steps.

"After your dream did you sleep well? I was sure I would have some nightmare about Gruge but I slept very well. I was about to go find you two when you showed up, I wondered if you had left me to go downstairs already. I've been reading for hours. I finally found a fairly normal book, something about taking care of the Iverly bat. We need to go eat I'm famished."

Max and Sam laughed at her zest. She had entertained them with her chatter all the way down to the last set of stairs. They'd never seen her look so happy.

"Well, aren't you guys hungry too?"

"Yes, let's go." Sam smiled. They sprinted down the final set of stairs. In the main hallway, Dramid stood waiting for them. "I trust your quarters were suitable and you slept well." He looked from one to the other. "I see you found the clothing left for you, they are adequate I hope." The three nodded in appreciation.

"We slept great, these feel comfortable." Max held out the long cape, "and now we're starving!" Max announced as they walked to the doors of the dining hall. "It's nice having an appetite again; I think I'm already gaining weight," he added rubbing his stomach.

Dramid turned to leave. "Enjoy your meal I shall return when you are finished." With a slight nod he retreated. The dining area was quiet and smelled enticing. They ate and visited about the pile of wood outside, which turned out to be the makings of a huge bonfire for the Christmas Eve party. They learned that piece of information from one of the other students, a shy young girl with curly black hair.

"That was rather odd; she wouldn't even look at us." Tracie remarked.

The three of them made very short work of devouring two platefuls each of breakfast.

It wasn't long before Dramid returned and stood at the entrance of the dining hall. Dramid and Beuffus seemed to always know when to arrive; they had done a very good job at making Max and his friends feel welcome.

Max stood, rubbed his full stomach and approached Dramid. "Uh, Dramid I just wanted to say thanks for everything; we're having a good time. When we go back will you and Beuffus be going with us?" Max looked up at Dramid as though he had all the answers to Max's many questions.

Dramid placed his hand on Max's shoulder, "Yes, we will be the ones to take you back. I sense some deeper question you want to ask."

Dramid was capable of perceiving everything in Max's mind; he would hardly be able to lie.

"Yeah, um was it you and Beuffus who helped me with everything while I was there? I've been thinking about it and I can remember back small things that happened which seemed to help me out of some pretty big jams. The night in the library, the math room, and other times, it made me wonder how much you actually helped. If we have to go back there, how much can you actually, uh well, make it more bearable— you know?"

"I know exactly what you are talking about. However, I cannot do a great deal of intervening, as it would draw too much attention to you. The question of did I help you? I assume you are referring to that night in the English room when the deplorable Mrs. Rosenblam made you copy sentences. Yes that was I, the airplane in Math however was Beuffus, he can be very — creative at times. Yes, we did lend you a hand as much as possible. Truth of the matter is you did a portion of it yourself and in the future you will be able to do more for yourself but by doing so you must be extremely careful. We will explain more about that soon enough."

Dramid seemed relaxed and in a good mood, so Max decided to raise the question he'd been waiting to ask. "Dramid, do you…?"

"I am truly sorry, Max, but you can't stay here longer than five days. We'd be happy having you here, but it just can't be. I'll explain that later also."

"How is it possible that you always know what I'm thinking?"

"Because I do," Dramid looked unblinkingly at Max then continued. "You remember that night on the stairs when I was a bat; you knew what I said to you just by my thinking it. I was rather impressed you could do that so soon. It stands to reason there are strong powers going on in you. It will all make sense when we are able to sit you down and give you the information. Trust me, we will tell you all the details soon enough. For now go outside and have some fun."

"Uh, yeah. One of the girls said they are building a bonfire for the party. Do you think the others will care if we help out?" Max asked.

"They would be happy to have you help. We can't expect you to learn our ways if you stand around all day talking with me. You can take this opportunity to meet some very interesting students. So, go on, get out of here."

Dramid didn't have to tell him twice. Max motioned to his friends who had stood back to allow him some private time with Dramid. They joined Max and headed for the front doors. Dramid followed close behind.

Outside on the top step they inhaled the cold air and watched the activities with interest. As they spoke a commotion arose in the center of the yard. Two slate gray wolves; nearly the size of ponies, converged onto the yard sending students in every direction huddling for cover and watching what the wolves had discovered.

"What do you suppose they have found?" Beuffus asked as he stopped beside Dramid, a look of inquiry on his confident face.

"The question would be who they found," Dramid corrected with keen interest.

"Mm yeah I see now. Come to think of it, I have never seen that boy before." Beuffus's eyes narrowed as the gray wolves pulled out from the crowd a tall, slender, evil looking boy appearing to be older, very disheveled, and grimy. He was held in the wolves' teeth with a vice like grip. The golden yellow eyes of the fierce beasts darted here and there while their prey screamed profanities and furious ramblings. He kicked at the air receiving no benefit; he was dragged mercilessly through the yard, down across the open bridge and finally deposited outside on the steps of the shabby cottage that stood on the outskirts of the castle.

"I'll have to have a look at that later," Dramid said somewhat preoccupied by the demonstration. He looked at Max, noticing the startled expression. "Not to worry my boy, the wolves were simply carrying out the trash. You see that uh," he paused. "Well I hesitate to guess exactly what it was. Unquestionably not the innocent boy it appeared to be, most assuredly a messenger for the enemy. No matter what or who Ms. Regunda Demora will get to the bottom of it."

"Those animals, the wolves, are they dangerous?" Max asked still a bit stunned regardless of the half -baked explanation.

"They are only dangerous to those who deserve it. We keep several roaming the grounds and many more wander the town and countryside. They are by far the best judge of character, wouldn't you say Beuffus?"

"Huh, oh yeah, by far they have a knack for—" Beuffus's attention was on the sky above, he sounded preoccupied. Then suddenly, he motioned in the direction above while elbowing Dramid in the arm. Without delay Dramid said, "Max, I want you to back up slowly and enter the castle, take Sam and Tracie with you." Judging by Dramid's cold, level voice, there was no time for twenty questions, they hastily did as they were told.

When they passed through the threshold, Max slowed his pace and stopped dead in his tracks, something was wrong; he felt a chill run up his spine and an intense pain cramped his right arm and hand. He was standing inside the castle rubbing his arm and staring out the open doors into the yard. Dramid stood outside on the top step assessing the danger. Suddenly Dramid turned on his heel, and in three very long strides he caught Max by the shoulder holding him still. "Max, we need to go now," he whispered.

"Go where, what's going on?"

Dramid steered Max towards the staircase. A loud howl came from outside and a pack of students ran into the building, sweeping past a dumb-founded Max while they took the steps two at a time. Some of them rushed to bar the windows, others prepared to lock the doors, still more ran around inside, through doors hidden under the steps. Several adults directed traffic, sending the students this way and that to shut down areas of the castle. Norman came by with a wood cart full of boards to bar the doors.

Sam and Tracie stood rooted to the spot, unable to move out of fear and disbelief. Max heard Dramid's booming voice enter his dazed mind from somewhere behind him. "We must not waste any more time. You three follow me now—and quickly!"

The group practically flew up the steps, two at a time, with Dramid in the lead, all the way up to Count Triad's office. People were already in the office, staring at the glass globes shouting numbers and information Max didn't understand.

Count Triad greeted them from the back of the room. "Hello, youngsters. I'm sorry for this disruption, but we must get you to a safe place. Come this way."

The Count guided them into a room at the back of his office. The door was at least three feet thick, there were no windows, just a comfortable looking couch and some soft squishy chairs; the walls were bare. A sturdy table sat in the center of the room, on it a round, glass ball like the ones in the Count's office sat shimmering with silver and brown lights. An awesome golden bat, at least a foot long, hung upon a peg sticking out of the rock wall. Its dark green eyes watched the trio with unperturbed curiosity.

Looking at Max, the Count stated forcefully, "You'll need to stay put until we come back. You'll find books, games, and other entertainment under that couch over there." He pointed. "I'm truly sorry, but we need to guard you and your friends for your safety. I'm sure you can understand."

"Yeah, sure, but what are we being guarded against?"

"We shall return, hopefully soon." The thick door closed on them. Max felt an irrational feeling of dread grip him.

"What do you suppose is going on out there?" Sam studied Max with a concerned look. Tracie also stared at Max, as though he could give them the answers. Simply put, he knew no more than they did. Or did he? Could he really read Dramid's mind or was it only when Dramid took the form of a bat?

Max looked at his two anxious friends, "I wonder if I could read Dramid's mind? Dramid said I could read his mind as a bat. Maybe I can do it when he's human." He sat on the plush velvet sofa while Tracie and Sam settled into nearby chairs where they could watch him. Max closed his eyes, feeling like a sideshow act.

He forced himself to concentrate on Dramid. His mind searched, he brought up the image of Dramid's face, the cool superiority, brilliant deep green eyes, and thick black hair. Max's breathing grew faster, his pulse quickened. Although there were no windows in the room, gradually he began to see outside onto the castle grounds.

Chaos filled the yard; it had become a meeting place for huge, ugly, flying creatures as they united over the lawn. They were four feet tall, some even larger; their enormous wingspan reached at least fourteen feet across. They had nearly human faces; except for their eye sockets which were sunken, leaving prominent pointy cheek bones. Their cloudy white eyes with black mirrored pupils were suspended in their skulls. Max could see the fierce look in the revolting beasts' eyes. Long hairy arms held various weapons. Their legs had long talons with vice grip claws. One of the creatures shrieked and plummeted to the ground, a spear sticking out of its chest.

Men dressed in full armor were protecting the castle. They surrounded the castle on all levels as they flung spears and shot flaming arrows at the invaders. One of the men pulled out a long sword and sliced off one of the wings of the invaders. Now flying with one wing, the creature tried desperately to continue his attack when another of its own kind grabbed it in its long talons and began ripping it to shreds. Body parts cluttered the ground. The others ignored it, but the angry gleam in their eyes grew stronger. They darted around the windows as though trying to find a way inside. Each time they drew closer they retreated with flaming arrows or spears sticking out of their bodies. Black bats fought the attackers in the air. They surrounded three of the wicked creatures landing on them and gnawing through the bodies, blood spilled heavily from the open wounds and the ugly things fell limply to the ground.

Max saw the horses from the game the night before, but this time they were ridden by skeleton-like creatures with long strips of flesh hanging off them. Their eyes were blood red; a few had several arrows and spears sticking through their empty bones. They pulled out the spears and threw them with extreme accuracy at their flying adversaries. They rode the horses with perfected ease, their white teeth gnashing the air, they shot arrows and stabbed at the invaders with long spears. Max suddenly felt himself grab at a creature that had descended on him; he twisted the neck and pulled as the body fell several floors down to the cluttered yard and flopped onto the ground. Now, his hands were bleeding from long gashes left there by the talons. In his mind he looked at the bloody wounds. They were not his hands at all, but the hands of Dramid.

Dramid was in trouble.

Sam and Tracie tried frantically to get Max's attention. He was turning red sweat dripped from his hairline and his breathing became rapid. This all combined with his dazed eyes that now stared at his hands alarmed his friends. "Max wake up, Max." Sam shouted while Tracie shook him.

Max felt dizzy. His mind was racing; his heart pounding, salty sweat ran into his eyes, stinging them. Sam reached out to catch him as he rocked forward, nearly falling off the couch.

The scene before Max was fixated within him. He couldn't find his way back to the little room. A rough voice came from somewhere and he was lifted off the couch, dangling in the air. He could see himself. Dramid shook him.

Gradually, Max came back to the room. Dramid stood there holding him high in the air shaking him forcefully.

Waking slightly from the trance, Max Tilted his head, and looked into Dramid's green, threatening eyes.

"Very impressive, my boy, but don't ever do that again! Do you understand me? It's far too dangerous for you until you learn to master it." Releasing Max he dropped him back to the couch and strode from the room. Large drops of fresh red blood remained behind on the floor.

Sam and Tracie rushed to Max flinging themselves beside him on the couch. Sam looked at Max with fear in his eyes.

"Wow, what happened?"

Max rubbed his eyes and swiped at the sweat on his forehead. Still a bit breathless, he declared knowingly, "It's a war. These huge flying creatures are attacking the castle outside." He pointed to the outer wall. "I couldn't stop once I was in his thoughts. I couldn't get out. Somehow he must have known."

"Yeah, he got mad when he came in and told you to stop and you couldn't. You were turning blue like you couldn't breathe or something, so he picked you up, shook you, and yelled at you."

"He looked real worried, like you were in danger," Tracie added.

Max shook his head. "I felt like I was never going to come back. I was lost in his thoughts."

"How do you feel now? Your color is getting better." Tracie stood, and walked to the door, following the trail of blood. Bending down, she looked closer at it.

"I'm fine! Don't be such a mother hen." Max blurted.

"So sorry for worrying about you grouch, but we were scared." Tracie huffed back. "And if you're so fine, where did this come from?" She pointed to the drying blood.

"It must have been true then," Max jumped up and bent down to feel the red splashes on the floor. "I saw Dramid kill one of those ghastly creatures, but in the process he was cut by its claws. It was a real mess out there. I don't know, but they may send us back to the orphanage after this, especially as mad as Dramid was."

Max sat back down on the couch and bent over, his head resting in his hands. "Then again they may not have to. If we're under attack, there may not be anything left when the fight is over. I wonder what they're fighting about. Those things on the horses were so revolting, like—living skeletons. They had big, bulging eyes and huge teeth. Their bones had dried up flaps of skin hanging off them, but they were on our side. I think. They were fighting the flying things that had human faces."

Tracie grimaced. "No wonder you were in a cold sweat. That sounds dreadful. Who was winning?"

"I'm not sure. I saw a pile of the rivals lying on the ground with spears sticking out of them, there were wings, heads and other dismembered parts, it was awful, and the skies were black with more coming."

They talked for more than an hour, unable to concentrate on anything other then the trouble outside. The room was completely soundproof, so they had no idea what was going on. Max felt drained from the episode. His nerves still tense, he managed to lie back on the couch and close his eyes. Because his visions were disturbing he rested only for a short time. He then paced the floor while Sam and Tracie carried on small talk, trying their best to include Max while another hour passed.

About the time Max thought he'd go crazy fearing the unknown, the click of the door lock alerted them. Dramid entered again, but the anger in his eyes had vanished, replaced by a warm greeting. "My boy, may we have a word with you in the outer room?" Glancing back at Tracie and Sam, Dramid bowed and said, "We won't be long, if you'll just be patient a few more minutes."

Max stood, feeling a bit like he was heading to the gallows. He gave a sideways glance at his friends and followed Dramid out the door. Max tried hard to get a look at the backs of Dramid's hands but they were moving too fast. The office was empty except for Count Triad who sat behind his desk. A pair of gray bats rested comfortably on each corner of the desk. He appeared to be studying a small glass globe.

As Max and Dramid approached the desk, the Count looked up with a warm smile, motioning to the chairs across the desk. "Have a seat Max."

Dramid pulled up a chair for himself and Max and they sat quietly waiting for the Count to finish what he was doing.

The Count cleaned his glass globe with a handkerchief. "I've heard of your earlier adventure in mind transfer. I must say, I'm quite impressed. I was fifteen before I could master even a portion of what you've done—and that was after two years of formal training. However, your actions could have been disastrous for you, had Dramid's superior vision not picked up on your escapade. I'm sure you could feel that. Now as you know the entire day has been a bit of a disaster, but things are calm and peaceful again. The other students are outside preparing for tonight's celebration and I feel you and your friends would benefit from being involved in that. I know I said earlier I wanted to give you some important information, but how about having some fun and waiting until tomorrow to have our talk?"

Max nodded, a little sigh of relief escaped his throat. He had been sure he was in trouble. "That sounds good. I could use some exercise after being cooped up all this time." There was a long uncomfortable pause before he continued. "Um, Sir, what were those things that attacked the castle?"

The Count smiled and shook his head, "Tomorrow we can have that conversation. Go have fun. You're safe and I have much work to do now." He managed a weak grin at Max, and then resumed studying the globe in his hands.

Dramid must have known the conversation was over, he stood and grabbed Max under the arm, pulling him up from the chair. "Go get your friends."

The Blazing Fire

CHAPTER FOURTEEN

Even after Max had done something they disapproved of he was still treated admirably. They had not punished him mercilessly. Max smiled he felt as though he belonged here with these strange people.

Max headed back to get Tracie and Sam, their patience was waning in the small cramped room; he paused and whispered to Dramid. "I'm really sorry for any problems I caused, thanks for saving me from myself."

"Just remember, never again, at least until you've had formal training, understand?" Dramid's eyes bore into Max waiting for acknowledgment. Max nodded, embarrassed he looked down at his feet, taking the opportunity to catch another glimpse of Dramid's hands. Dramid grinned lopsided. "Yes one of them managed to get in through the window where I was guarding the Count." He held up his hand showing the deep bloodied wounds. "I'll be fine, now go, get out of here."

Finally free, the three of them headed outside joining the others who were reconstructing the wood pile. The invaders had managed not only to darken the grounds with blood but to tear up the work that had been done. Jill ran over to welcome them and introduced them to several other students. A short, brown- haired boy about the same age as Jill walked up beside them; in his hand he carried a thin strip of copper like the one in Max's crate back at the school.

Max smiled at him. "Hi, my name is Max. What's yours?"

The youngster just shrugged and smiled.

"What do you have there?" Max asked, pointing to the strip.

"It's my triguard. It will help me if any more of those big ugly Vorax come back."

"How will it protect you from—what did you call them?"

"Vorax! They're a genetic invention of the Vlauds. They can fly in the daylight, but they hate the reflection off this copper—it melts their skin."

"Those are the things that just tried to get into the castle?"

The boy shook his head, "Oh, they weren't trying to get into the castle. They were trying to get to a kid who's inside the castle. He has the blood of one of the originals."

Beuffus interrupted, "is everyone having a good time?" He handed sharp sticks to Max, Tracie, and Sam. Max instinctively looked up in the sky to see if the sticks were intended to stab one of the creatures. Beuffus laughed. "These are to cook your dinner with.

It would have been lunch, but with all the commotion around here we're running behind schedule."

The puzzled look on Max's face made Beuffus laugh again he looked out at the others'. "See those kids over there? You go to that table and one of the ladies will help you."

The table held a wide array of raw meat, vegetables, fruit, cookies, bread, cheese, and a large barrel containing some type of bright green juice. Some of the kids were drinking two glasses at a time. They watched as the others reached into various trays of food, pulled out several combinations and slid them onto the stick then set them over hot coals to cook.

"Do you have any idea what you're doing?" Tracie turned in the direction of the voice. A tall stocky boy had walked up behind her with a mischievous grin spread across his wide face. His ball cap was pulled firmly on his head and his yellow green eyes sparkled. "Hi, I'm Markus," He held out his broad hand and smiled revealing a silver row of braces aligning his teeth. "You three are new here aren't you?"

"Yes we are," Tracie said shaking his hand. "As for your question of do we know what we're doing the answer is no, we haven't' the foggiest idea." She said.

"We're just visiting I'm Max this here is Sam" Max said shaking the bigger boy's bulky hand.

"Let me show you how this goes." Markus held up his stick and began shoving the food onto it. Then he held it over the blazing hot fire pit and in seconds it was cooked to perfection. The rest of them did the same and they began eating a hot meal outside in the cold.

"What's this green juice?" Max asked the tall woman who stood behind the table filling cups full of the liquid.

"It comes from the gaba berry tree—a tree that grows bright green berries the size of walnuts. They contain powerful vitamins and a compound that helps those who drink it to see in the dark for an hour or two. We smash the berries to make this punch. Then we serve it on special occasions when it's necessary to see in the dark. Do you like it?"

"Uh, yeah it's pretty good." Max said holding out his cup for the woman to refill it.

Jill told Max that when they're dried, the berries turn into black stones having a smooth side and a rough side. Remembering the stone Gramps had given him, he wondered if it was a gaba berry.

"What do you do with them in the dried form?" He asked Jill.

"They're very powerful after they've dried, so all you have to do is put them in your mouth and they melt slowly. They help you see in the dark for a long time. They also help strengthen powers—if you have any. Around here, we dry them by the thousands and give them to the warriors and to the students." Jill said. She saw someone she knew and bounced off to play.

Max stared out at the others who were playing games, singing, and a few were still eating. A commotion of some kind began over near the edge of the grounds and everyone looked at the large stone building that housed the horses for Valentia, and—from the looks of things—a great many bats that were the size of housecats. The cloud of bats flew from the top door of the barn circling the grounds.

The spectacle was awesome; their huge black bodies blocked out the afternoon sun for a moment. Watching them land on the shoulders of students, Max hoped these bats were friendly. Beuffus came up behind him and said, "These bats each belong to a student. They are very loyal, alerting their owners of danger and keeping a vigilant eye on them like a pet wolf would. They also act as carriers, delivering items to and from."

"What are they doing now?" Max asked.

"They're collecting wish lists, which they'll carry home to the student's family or to a benefactor who'll fill the Christmas order. Then everyone will have a gift tomorrow."

Max sighed, wishing he had someone other than Tracie and Sam who cared enough to get him a gift. It didn't have to be anything big; just the fact that someone cared would be nice.

Bueffus gave him a sympathetic look. "Hey kid, look what's headed your way!" He pointed up in the sky as a bat with shiny brown eyes descended upon them. Instinctively, Max ducked.

Beuffus chuckled. "He can't land if you move. Sam, Tracie, hold still and let them land on your shoulders." Sam and Tracie were ducking and dodging, afraid of being injured by them. Finally the bats managed to land safely.

With a hint of amusement, Beuffus said, "Well done! Now all you have to do is get to know them. While you're here, they'll be your friends. You need to give them a name and tell them what you will call them. And tell them what you'd most like to receive for your gift tomorrow—within reason that is, of course you may not get what you ask for but it's worth a try."

Max started off. "Hi, my name is Max and I…"

"Max, you don't have to talk out loud. These bats can read your thoughts. Just think your conversation; they'll get it."

Max named his bat Dusk, Tracie named hers Flutter, and Sam called his Beast. They spent the next half hour thinking their wishes and chuckling about how strange it was. They made a mutual wish of wanting nothing more then to be able to stay forever.

As the sun disappeared below the horizon, the bats left the shoulders of their students and went in search of food they could feast on before they went to work delivering the students wish lists. The older students gathered around the pyramid, holding their capes aloft.

"What are they doing?" Max asked Beuffus while pointing to the students standing around the wood pile.

"They are using their powers to start the fire. Those are the older students. This is their opportunity to compare their powers—we can soon tell who has them mastered and who needs practice."

A tall red- haired girl shouted, and moments later a tiny flame crept over the wood in front of her. While some of the other students started similar spots on the pyramid which was now shimmering with several burning areas. A loud yelp came from a short blond girl who looked to be around fourteen. She backed away, squealing in pain, "Oops, oh gosh, ow owww!" Somehow she'd set her own foot ablaze.

Beuffus stepped around the crowd and with a wave of his hand the flame was out. She limped off over to where a woman dressed all in black, with long shining ebony hair sat astride a tall horse the color of the woman's attire. The wounded girl was lifted onto the horse and whisked away in a flurry of black. Beuffus assured them, "She'll be alright. This happens often."

Soon all of the small lit patches progressed to one very large blaze. The dry wood caught fire and the flames leapt into the air, forcing everyone to move back. The evening was filled with games and roasting Nighttail over the bonfire. Max learned this wonderfully sweet buttery tasting fruit grew in long cascades on tall trees; it was favored by the many bats that sucked the liquid contents from the hard shell. The Nighttail would then fall from the tree and by roasting them the meaty insides could be eaten by the students.

The most exciting of all was the soar through the air. Students lined up waiting their turns. They would sit down on large ox hides while several bats held the hide in their clawed grip and flew off into the night sky. Finally, they were returned safely to the ground after a few minutes of excitement. Max felt free and alive when he was flying up in the air. It was an awesome site to see several students floating around in the night sky all in different directions. The view from above made the castle look like a city.

Finally after all the students had finished their flight, they settled around the fire for a demonstration of magical powers displayed by an Elder—the castle repairman. Once he'd been a powerful professor and had taught students how to perform special counter-curses from enemies. Unfortunately, he had been out numbered in a violent battle and a curse got past him, causing him damage that no one could cure. He now had a meek and quiet demeanor; he'd forgotten more than others had ever known. He was still able to show the powers that remained, and perform for the students while taking exceptional care of the castle.

It was sad, Max thought but it was nice that the man was still honored and respected by everyone.

Time swept by; the students were mesmerized by the man's ability. His once-strong hands, now shaky and slow, could still perform amazing deeds. He made things appear and disappear then caught items on fire midair with a single wave of his hand. Heavy concentration brought on strange beasts, some fearsome, some kindly, and in a blink they were gone. Near the end of the performance Max's mind wandered. What were these people? How could all this be happening—and how was he involved?

He couldn't wait much longer for that talk with the Count.

A Midnight Ride

CHAPTER FIFTEEN

"Now students it's time for the grand finale." A booming voice echoed through the crowd. It had come from an enormous dark hooded outline standing next to the Elder.

The Elder stepped up and with open arms out to his sides he said. "Thank you all for being such a good audience. I hope that one day many of you will wish to entertain others as a part of sharing our unique talents." He spoke very slowly his voice a little shaky.

"I now give you Misty, our very dear friend".

Unexpectedly a cloud of blue, green, and maroon smoke appeared. As it cleared, a beautiful white horse stood before the crowd. The Elder bowed low as the noble animal trotted around the yard with its graceful tail streaming in the wind. At last her eyes came to rest on Max. Max felt the heat of embarrassment rise as the other students stared at him, and then they began clapping.

The horse stepped forward standing directly in front of Max, staring at him with warm brown eyes – telling him to climb aboard.

"What, now I can read horses thoughts?" He mumbled to himself the horse nodded slightly. The clapping and cheering increased in tempo.

Jill grabbed Max's arm and shook it with a great beaming smile. "Misty chose you! Climb on, and she'll take you for a journey into the night. It's the grand finale; only one student gets the ride during each gathering."

Max had been chosen to take the "night ride." He had ridden a few times in his life, but Gramp's out dated plow horses were nothing like this majestic animal. The mare nickered a soft welcome and bowed low for Max to mount. He touched her nose with his fingers and the warm softness gave him courage.

Max looked around at the other students who were chanting "go go go go." He knew that if he didn't go, he would disappoint not only this unusual animal but every student in the yard. He also didn't want to look like a coward. He took a deep breath and slid his leg over her back. The students' clapping grew fainter as they left the activities far behind them and entered into the cold darkness. Max entwined his fingers in the long mane while Misty galloped through the fields. The darkness made the ride even more exciting. Max hoped the horse could see at night; his gaba juice had almost worn off. He could see eyes shining through the grass and from behind trees. He wondered what or who they belonged to.

The full moon appeared from behind a big cloud, sparkling on a shallow river in front of them. The big mare leapt into the water and trotted through it, sending ice cold splashes onto Max's face. He laughed, feeling invigorated. When Misty reached the other side, she climbed the bank and slowed her pace while entering a grove of trees, she was careful not to scrape her passenger off on the low-hanging branches. From the darkest recess of the forest, Max saw the glimmer of a faint light. A few minutes later, Misty walked into a clearing lit by lanterns and bustling with activity. Ten or more horses like Misty stood to one side, eating hay. In the center of the clearing several large wolves lay chewing on long red bones keeping a watchful eye out for danger. They stared briefly at Max and Misty then continued the assault on the bones.

A tall man with scars on his face limped toward them. Max grabbed the mane in fear, but a reassuring nicker from Misty told him all was well. A deep, growling voice filled the night air, and the dark outline of the man grew closer.

"Are ye having a good ride for yourself, young man?"

"Yes, sir," Max managed to mumble a few words then he swallowed hard.

"Good, good! That mare will take good care of you. My name's Mervin, I tend to all these horses, the wolves, and various other critters."

"My name is Max, sir. It's nice to meet you."

"Not sir – just call me Mervin. Nice to meet you then, Max." Mervin nodded and went about his duties, caring for the animals. Max watched Mervin resume stitching up three deep gashes across the back of a wolf pup. The pup lay there quietly while Mervin talked calmly to it. He worked with steady hands in a slow methodic manner to doctor the injured animal. Max didn't have the time to ask questions even though he was curious about the wound. Misty gave him no more time as she trotted off.

Once again, she galloped off into the unknown. In the moonlight, Max could see a stone wall looming before them. He held tight; and closed one eye then the other as it appeared they were going to either go over or through the wall. He felt himself rise into the air and he opened his eyes, the leap over the wall seemed endless. When they finally hit ground again, Max's stomach felt as though it had lodged in his throat. They raced downhill toward a speck of light in the distance. Max could scarcely see due to his watering eyes from the cold air. They slowed their descent giving Max the opportunity to wipe his eyes with his sleeve. All he could see was an enormous pile of brush that Misty ducked her head and pushed through.

They had entered a cave that had been cleverly hidden by the underbrush. Squeezing through the narrow opening Max was astonished to see they had entered a town. The streets of stone were full of small horses and the tiny people who rode them where dressed in bright colors. Small shops with doors standing open had miniature people racing in and out, carrying packages. Small cart horses pulled tiny wagons to and fro – the tiny drivers wore top hats which they tipped in Max's direction. Colored lights adorned all the little shops, and music played in the streets.

Max watched as the little town bustled with activity. Smiles and waves from its inhabitants made him feel welcome. Children playing in the streets were riding insects that resembled cockroaches; only they were gigantic compared to the children. The bugs seemed to have as much fun as the youngsters, it was an implausible display.

Max thought he and Misty must look huge to these people, yet no one seemed to mind his presence. Max was so busy looking at the bright colors and the scurrying people that he didn't notice the sign hanging above the main street of town. As Misty passed under the sign, it smacked Max on the forehead stunning him for a second and he nearly fell off. Misty stopped while Max rocked back from the blow. Recovering, he held his throbbing head. He heard a giggle next to the left of him. Standing on a long ladder almost level with Max, stood an old woman in a festive blue, pink, and violet gown with an orange scarf tied around her gray hair. The mare tossed her head and softly pawed the ground, the little lady handed Max a handkerchief, and in a squeaky voice said, "Oh my, I did conk you on the head, I was simply trying to hang the new sign and you just came up too fast. Well ain't that the limit, there seems to be a bump there on your forehead." She pointed her tiny finger at Max's head.

"That's okay." Max smiled holding his hand up to the small welt. Looking at the lady up close, she couldn't have been two feet tall; she was only as big around as his arm.

"So you're the lucky rider chosen for the adventure? We see a rider once in awhile during their special gatherings. Are you enjoying your ride?"

"Yes, it's a little scary, but fun. Where am I?"

"Oh, dear that whack on the head has caused your memory to lapse. I am truly sorry." The small woman looked as though she were going to cry.

"Uh, No, nothing like that. I'm actually new to the area I just arrived yesterday so I didn't exactly know this place existed."

"Well, thank goodness. I was afraid I had knocked you senseless. This is Sparkwood, our home. We are the Tavian people. Our town was saved by the Vamparians, so we formed a special relationship. Once a year, we all get together and have a huge feast. We're very thankful to your people, and we express our gratitude by keeping an eye out for danger and sending warnings if we see anything unusual."

Max nodded, "This is a nice town."

"Yes, well, we greet our night riders with a rest and a drink." The little lady bounced off the ladder, trotted over to the café. She returned with a large, steaming mug topped with frothy sweet cream. "This is hot gaba shiva juice. It will not only help you see in the dark for the rest of the trip, but will also keep you nice and warm, thanks to the powdered shiva vine I put in for you."

Max accepted the drink with a smile. It would be nice to see in the dark, his gaba juice had worn off completely. He learned the woman's name was Norma; she was a charming hostess. They spent nearly half an hour visiting until Misty pawed the ground a bit more anxiously, warning him it was time to leave. Max downed the rest of the sweet liquid.

"Well, I suppose we must go. Thank you, Norma. I hope to see you again."

"You will, my dear boy, you will. Enjoy the rest of your trip. And watch out for low hanging signs." She winked and with a wave of her petite hand, she bound back up the ladder.

They were off again, leaving the little town far behind, the adventure nearing the end. Max sniffed the cool night air, treasuring every second of the ride. He felt alive and happy. Norma had been right – he didn't feel the cold, and now he could see shapes around him as though it were only twilight.

As they neared the forest again, Max saw movement out of the corner of his eye. When he turned to look, something struck the middle of his back. Seconds later, another hit. "Misty, something's throwing stuff at me! Ouch!" Yet another object hit his hand; he caught it as it rolled down his leg. The object appeared to be a nut of some kind.

Misty stopped and turned, then gave a loud whinny and shook her head. A group of round, hairy creatures scurried deeper into the dense forest, chattering and giggling in deep bubbling voices.

"What were those things?" Max concentrated on Misty's thoughts so he could receive her answer.

A soft voice replied, "Those were Drillo children, young and naughty. They're furry people who live in these woods. The adults are friendly if they know you won't harm them, but the children are full of mischief."

"Harmless, hah! I'm sure I have welts on my back right now."

"I am sorry, Max. I should have been faster through these woods; I thought it was late enough that they'd be sleeping."

It suddenly dawned on Max that the horse had actually talked to him. She spoke actual words he had heard them and not telepathically either.

"Hey you talked, how do you do that?"

"The same way you do that; I just open my mouth and speak."

"Yes, but horses can't talk."

"Who says we can't? Haven't you noticed there are no such rules here in our land?"

"So you've been quiet all this time when we could have been talking?"

"I wanted you to enjoy the ride without being interrupted."

"Yes, but now I don't feel so alone, where do we go from here, how much longer until we get back?"

"That's another reason I don't let passengers know I talk. I must concentrate on getting you back safely and not on your questions, so please excuse me while I transport you to the castle. We aren't far now."

Riding the horse in the moonlight left Max's legs sore and his backside even sorer. He was grateful to Misty for her tour but he was ready for the bed upstairs in the warm, comfortable room.

As they neared the campfire, he saw the flames had turned to red embers and was surrounded by a heap of ash. Nearly all of the other students had retreated to their rooms, but his faithful friends, accompanied by Beuffus, waited on a hollow log near the spent fire.

Misty kindly lowered herself to the ground for Max to dismount. He patted her and whispered, "Thanks for the great adventure, girl."

"It was my pleasure, young Max. My first passenger was your mother many years ago. You are as polite as she was." Misty nickered softly, and then trotted away with her tail flipping this way and that. Max stood glued to the spot. This was the second time someone had mentioned his mother. Now he had a dozen more questions forming in his mind.

His friends came running up to him, firing questions.

"Where did you go?"

"What did you do?"

"Was it fun?"

"Weren't you scared out there in the dark so long?"

"We were worried about you."

"Beuffus told us the trip took a long time and you'd be fine."

"I was fine. I had a lot of fun, but I didn't realize we'd been gone nearly —what time is it anyway Beuffus?"

"Beuffus smiled you've been gone nearly three hours. Its two o'clock in the morning. We better get you three in to bed."

Max stepped delicately, "my legs feel like rubber and my behind is— well, thankful that the ride is over."

Laughing, they all entered the castle. Beuffus ruffled Max's hair and grinned. "Well then, you three had better get some sleep. We will have another busy day tomorrow."

"Thanks, Beuffus, for everything."

"No problem, kid. Good night."

"Good night," they all chimed. Walking up the long stairs, Max began recounting his adventure to his friends, his saga continued while they sat in the commons, leaving nothing out.

Max knew they needed to get some sleep yet the evening's excitement had them wound up. It was nearly three in the morning by the time they finished matching stories about the last couple of days and meeting some of the other students. An hour later they where all snug and warm in their beds.

A Great Christmas.

CHAPTER SIXTEEN

What seemed like a very short time later, the bright sunlight poked through the unshuttered window forcing Max awake. His pleasant dreams were gone, he was so tired he could hardly open his eyes, yet the noise outside drew his attention. He staggered to the window and looked out. Kids and teachers were scattered across the lawn, playing and laughing. The excitement was contagious. Max shook Sam awake and they quickly dressed and hurried off to find Tracie.

At the entrance to the girls' room, Brugo appeared, his big broom piling dirt on the stone floor.

"Well good morning to you, boys. If you're lookin' for Tracie, she left awhile ago, saying something about being hungry enough to eat a horse."

"Thanks, Brugo." The boys traipsed down the hall. They too were hungry, but not enough to eat a horse – especially after an evening spent with Misty. When they reached the top of the steps, they remembered this was Christmas morning. That explained why the other kids were racing around with boxes and interesting gadgets.

Max and Sam headed straight for the dining room, where they found Tracie, Jill, and Markus— who had taken an instant liking to Tracie due to her quiet kindness. They were eating eggs and bacon with fruit. Between bites, Tracie said. "Good morning, guys. I was going to wake you, but figured you needed your sleep."

"I could have slept all day, but I forgot to close the shudders when I went to bed and the sun was bright this morning." Max said as he set off to gather his meal. He felt a tingle of excitement, remembering this was the day he'd get answers to his questions. As he walked past the back table, the sandy-haired boy whose name was Biff Duncan the same boy who'd given him a wicked look on his first day bitterly taunted Max between bites of toast.

"Well, well, if it isn't the sniveling little orphan from nowhere who has the supposedly all powerful blood."

Max stopped and turned, he looked at the five boys as though he wanted to say something. He wanted to ask them what their problem was – he hadn't done anything to them. On the other hand, why should he lower himself to their level? So he continued walking and ignored them. Beuffus, who was standing in the doorway, noticed the exchange and gave Biff – a disapproving grimace with a narrowing of his eyes. Max smiled, at seeing Biff fidget in his seat and look down at his plate of food.

Beuffus walked up to Max's table. "Did you three get enough sleep?"

"We could have slept more, but we're up now." Sam yawned.

"You had a late night last night. But today is a very exciting day for all of you." Max nodded his agreement then gave Beuffus a somber glance. "What's with that kid over there, why is he so unfriendly? He said I had supposedly powerful blood? What does that mean?"

Beuffus waved a hand.

"Oh, Biff Duncan is a bit of an obnoxious kid he tries hard to cause trouble. His father was the same way. They believe banishment of the older blood will eventually cause our kind to be soft and fearful. We'll explain it later today after you three open your gifts. Sam and Tracie can enjoy the celebration while we fill you in on a lifetime of knowledge. Finish eating and we'll get started."

It didn't take long for the three of them to finish breakfast, especially since they were suddenly the last three students in the great dining hall. The commotion and laughter outside called to them. Stepping out the front door, they entered a flurry of activity with more strange items, games, and gadgets than they'd ever seen in one place.

"Whoa!" Sam sighed.

"Do you believe this?" Tracie asked breathlessly.

"Not if I hadn't seen it for myself!" Max ducked as a toy bat zoomed over his head.

The same bats that had come to rest on their shoulders the night before wove and darted through the crowd, carrying strangely etched boxes in their clawed feet. The bats flapped their wings in steady sweeps; they offered the packages they carried to Sam and Tracie.

"Wow, thanks Flutter." Tracie reached out to stroke the bats head. Tracie wasted no time tearing at the tightly tied vine that held the lid in place.

Sam told Beast he was impressed by his flight maneuvers while carrying such a large package.

Max stared curiously at the little rolled-up paper Dusk had brought him. Tracie squealed with delight as she opened a box that contained a gold necklace with a crystal locket; it was the most intense color of blue she had ever seen. Tracie lifted the locket and peered closely. She sat down in awe and began to read the detailed instructions:

> *This crystal charm is rare it is meant for those who*
> *from time to time feel alone, it will provide you with a sense of*
> *self as you conjure an image. Stand before a mirror, hold*
> *the crystal facing the mirror, imagine a friend standing*
> *before you, she will appear for your eyes only.*

> *Enjoy with warmest regards,*
> *the Vamparian people.*

Sam watched Tracie for a while, and then he tore into the brown wood box with black, burnt etchings of bats, spears and reptiles; a plain old ordinary pair of glasses lay in the box, they were very small glasses with tiny lenses "Um a pair of glasses," they looked fairly common. Sam turned them around upside down, sideways and he still had no idea what he was to use them for since he did not wear glasses. Hanging from the side of the glasses was a white tag.

"When all else fails read the directions," Sam muttered to himself.

"This will be a wonderfully fun gift for you. We know
it will seem very strange, and will take some getting used to.
Also understand they cannot and will not hurt you; don't be alarmed
as
there are many of them. This is a ghost finder, yes ghost.
They can be very entertaining to watch.
Enjoy,
Your friends, the Vamparian people."

Sam and Tracie fell silent as they noticed that Max had no gift – just a paper scroll he'd unrolled. He read the contents, looked up at them both, then lowered his head and read the contents of the scroll to them.

"This says it's time to learn my true identity, and that I'll receive my gift in the chambers of Count Triad." Max looked up from his paper; his gaze swept past his friends to Dramid, who stood in the doorway of the castle.

"Shall we go?" Dramid asked serenely.

With an excited, yet fearful look to his friends, Max dashed off to his next adventure, leaving Sam and Tracie in the yard with their new gifts and hundreds of excited students, teachers, bats and a variety of bizarre creatures.

"I hope it goes well for Max," Tracie watched as he disappeared through the doors.

"Yeah, I hope so too." Sam said distractedly while trying desperately to detach the instruction tag from his gift. "I don't know Trace, but these are by far the weirdest gifts I've ever received."

"Yeah, check this out." Tracie held up her necklace and instructions so Sam could look. With baffled looks in each other's direction, they tinkered with their gifts for part of the morning.

The Talk with the Count

CHAPTER SEVENTEEN

Dramid placed his hand on Max's shoulder as they stopped at the bottom of the long stairway leading to Count Triad's office. "This is the moment you've been waiting for. I hope you can take it all in and still remain a good-hearted young man."

Max looked up at Dramid and nodded, not exactly sure how some news about himself could change his behavior.

Dramid evidently caught this particular thought and replied. "Sometimes a person's supremacy goes to their head and it can cause evil instead of good." Max gave him a reasonably blank look.

Dramid sighed. Max would not understand until he knew the truth. "Okay then, you undoubtedly are ready, let's go." They marched up the steps.

Max's heart beat faster and his breath rushed into his lungs. He had waited a long time to get answers and now that it was about to happen, he actually wanted to turn an about face and run back outside.

Dramid looked down at him, "No need to be nervous. I know it's frightening, but for the most part we have good news."

Max managed a shaky smile and Dramid laughed and clapped him on the back. "You almost convinced me with that half-smile."

That made Max smile for real. The humor in Dramid's voice reassured him. Reaching the tall wooden door, Dramid gave Max a quick once over. "All right?"

"All right," Max nodded. The enormous door was the last barrier to his questions and their answers. He swallowed hard, finding his mouth entirely to dry to function. The hall was dim and the chill in the castle made him wrap his cape tighter around himself. Dramid stepped up and grabbed at the huge ring in the center of the door.

The door groaned and they stepped inside. The room seemed different than Max remembered from a few days earlier; it was darker and the round glass balls that had been filled with lights, flashes, and pictures were now calmly reflecting the warm fire. Max took in everything, trying to commit the room's contents to memory for later daydreaming. The door shut behind them with a thud. The room was silent except for the sound of the wood snapping in the fire and the occasional screech of the bats lining the beams sleeping the day away.

"Come right in, my dear boy," the Count's voice boomed at them, yet he wasn't in sight. Dramid directed Max by the shoulder toward the back of the room. Seated behind the same desk he had been sitting at when Max had first met him, the Count motioned toward two velvet chairs. "Have a seat. It's good to see you again, Max. I hope your stay with us has been agreeable."

Now that he was with the Count, Max wondered why he'd been so afraid. The man's deep black eyes were settling to Max, and his warm smile was evidence of his kind demeanor.

"Yeah," Max said, and cleared his throat. "Yes sir. This has been the best time in my life."

"I trust your friends are also enjoying themselves." Count Triad asked with one raised eyebrow.

"Yes sir, very much. Thank you."

"Good! That's the least that we can do. Now, I know this is Christmas, so in your tradition, I guess a Merry Christmas is in order. We celebrate a little differently, as you can see. We don't go overboard with it, but we make sure the students have a good time." He reached into the desk drawer, produced a box, and handed it to Max.

"This is your gift, Max. We'll need to explain what it is – that's why I wanted to give it to you in private."

Max accepted the box; he tipped it a bit to see if it rattled. "Thanks"

The box was very small and made of wood. On the top and sides it had the same type of etchings as Sams gift had. It had black bats, wolves, a full moon; and a dagger or two; the images preoccupied Max.

229

His eyes were wide with wonder. He felt happy that someone cared enough to think of him.

Dramid and Count Triad exchanged a smile at the boy's innocent enjoyment.

"Well, are you going to open it or not?" Dramid asked.

"Oh, yeah!" Max looked at the lid and turned the box, there was a small brass latch which he unhooked and lifted the lid, revealing a flat stone with a surface similar to the round glass balls that adorned the shelves and tables in that very room. He looked up at the Count, amazed.

"Wow! Thank you – but, um sir, what is it?"

Again, both men chuckled. The Count answered.

"That is a viewer. We can see most everything in ours; yours will allow you to view us here at the castle. We know you can't stay with us, so we want you to be able to see us. As you look into its depths, let your thoughts reproduce some part of the castle. If done correctly, you'll be able to see a present-time view of that area. You must keep a pure mind and have no other thoughts, or it may be jumbled. As you practice, this will get easier." He held up a hand, anticipating Max's next question.

"No one but you can create a picture in it; only someone with the right powers can make it work. To most people, this is a glass stone and nothing else. Yet, dear boy, in the wrong hands, it will become so hot it can scorch a human hand. Therefore, it must stay hidden to avoid injury; we have made it small enough to fit in your pocket so you will need to keep it concealed."

Max nodded. "Thank you very much. I'll keep it safe."

"Now then, shall we begin our little chat?" The Count leaned back in his chair, resting his chin on his index finger and thumb, concentrating intensely. Finally after several moments he spoke.

"I believe we need a little help with this one." He stood and approached the far wall and pulled a cord revealing a hole in the stone wall far above his head. The bottom of a staircase could be seen suspended above. He reached up to pull it down.

Dramid hurried to his side. "Let me help you, Triad."

"Thank you." The Count nodded.

As Dramid pulled the steps down, the Count beckoned Max forward. "Come on then, let's go on up and have a look around." They climbed the steep stairway and entered a darkened room.

From one corner Max heard a snoring noise. "What is that?" He whispered.

"Oh that is just Foxi, she is my dear old pet, and a very good mouser. Even the smart mice can't fool her." Dramid snapped his fingers and the lamps lit the room, in the dim light Max watched the Count gently stroking the back of the largest black cat he'd ever seen. She lay carelessly on a short book case. Stretched out as she was she must have been four feet long, and very plump.

Max stared disbelievingly at her and stood still as though he may be her next supper. "Is she a panther?"

The Count chuckled, "Oh, goodness no! She's just a big, fat cat." Hearing his words, the cat growled deep in her throat and blinked her amethyst colored eyes. The Count shrugged. "Sorry about the reference to your size, my dear, but you could stand a little more exercise and a lot less napping."

The cat yawned and stretched, her long sharp claws raking the top of the book case.

The Count motioned to the end of the table nearest the bookcase "Let's sit here so we can get a visual." He guided Max to a table with eight chairs around it. He pulled down a round viewer that was suspended above; as it came to rest, it took up one entire end of the table.

"This particular viewer shows the past." Dramid said.

"Shall we begin then?" The Count leaned back in his chair.

"As you may have already guessed, we're different than typical humans. I know you've wondered all along why you can do certain things, such as read other people's thoughts and communicate your own thoughts without speaking. And why you have been witness to our people who can carry fire in their hands disappear and reappear and so on and so fourth"

Max nodded, his eyes never leaving the Count as he continued. "We, as well as yourself, are Vamparians. We descended from vampires many years ago." The silence was deafening, Max felt a dizziness envelop him.

"I'm a, a vam-vam -vampire?" He stuttered, sitting up suddenly, while instinctively placing his thumb and forefinger on his two top canine teeth not believing his ears.

"Well, in a way. Many years ago, a man named Count Braqouls didn't have the stomach for the usual bloodsucking that the vampires are known for." A graphic image of a vampire in a black cape appeared in the viewer. The resemblance to the man in the painting back at the Orphanage was uncanny.

"Count Braqouls loved all mankind and animals as well, and refused to take a life to satisfy his hunger. So he and a friend by the name of Professor Vondrolier, known as the Doctor, worked to change the physical and mental aspects that caused them to be killers. The Count had to change his diet and fight the physical and mental need for blood. Luckily, he was successful, and the great doctor discovered the genetic material responsible for an array of vicious behaviors. Are you following me so far?" The Count peered up at Max.

"Yes, I think so," Max managed.

"Good, I'll continue. The test subjects were fifty vampire babies who were basically created in a lab by the Doctor. He made sure they had no need for blood, and he monitored their every move as they grew. Each of these subjects prospered. Many of their offspring began the little town we call Transfellula.

"One of these test subjects was your grandfather, Ben Von Dretti Morgan."

Max gulped as an image of Gramps appeared in the viewer, but the Count continued.

"Unlike true vampires, we don't live forever as walking dead – but we do live a very long time. We are much more vulnerable then the true vampire yet we are able to enjoy sunshine and garlic, and we eat food, not blood." The Count wrinkled his nose at the mention of drinking blood.

"Are you all right, my boy? You look a little pale. Would you like a cold fallot juice?" Dramid waved his hand, and a frosty mug of the familiar lavender juice appeared before Max. He welcomed the distraction; it gave him a few moments to digest what he'd just heard.

"As time went on, the good doctor realized the offspring of these subjects were good and still powerful. They were able to perform all of the same incredible feats of the unexplained that the vampires could. He opened the school to help all Vamparians understand and learn. Even some of the vampires who didn't have the stomach for the killing and drinking of blood came over to our side. And in time with the doctors help they too became like us. Dramid here is the son of one of the test subjects. Both of our fathers were test subjects, like your grandfather. However, our fathers met and wed actual Vampires who wished to be taken away from that life. Therefore, we are more powerful than some of the others. In fact, you, my friend, are the son of a most powerful Vampire—Count Viktar Von Dimitar. You don't carry his name, for your mother, the Countess Vallery Von Dretti Morgan, didn't wish to have you labeled as a vampire's son." The viewer showed a tall, handsome man with coal black, shoulder length hair and dark, cool eyes.

Max jumped up to his feet. "Is that my father?"

"Yes, the count said. And this is your mother." A lovely woman with deep clover green eyes and long wavy hair appeared in the viewer. Max stared at her for a long time.

"Your grandfather allowed his only daughter to give you – his only grandson – his family name. He was proud to have you."

"What about my father?" Max asked.

"Your father was a good man. His earlier misadventures only heightened your mother's interest in him. He went through a lot to be with her and lead a normal Vamparian life. You see, due to some of the unusual aspects of a Vampire's genetic makeup, the doctor had to give him, and anyone else wishing to change over, daily shots for nearly a year. The shots allowed him to withstand daylight and actually eat regular food instead of drinking blood. It was well worth it, because your father proved to be a most valuable asset to your family and the Vamparian kind. Unfortunately, by taking the shots to become one of us he was left a bit more vulnerable than the true vampire." Max was captivated by the scene unfolding in the viewer it was a tall man his black hair flowing as he fought with ultimate precision using a gold bladed sword.

"Is that my—my father there in that battle?" Max asked as he stared into the globe.

"Yes that's him. Your father was killed in a fierce battle at Mt. Dravon. He did, however, because of his courage and extreme fighting ability take many of the Vampire force with him when he died. His death was not in vain. Nevertheless, your Mother felt responsible since she'd been the reason for him to change over. You were born just ten days after his death. Your mother loved you very much, but she couldn't forgive herself for causing your father's death – even though she had nothing to do with it. He would have changed over anyway. His heart was much too big to kill and slaughter innocent people as the Vampires do."

Max felt the sting of tears come to his eyes. Now he knew about the mother and father he'd never known. Truthfully, he hadn't thought too much about them until now. Grandpa Ben had always been there for him, and had never talked about them. Now he understood why.

"He would have told you in his own good time, but I'm sure it brought distressing memories. Your grandfather loved both your mother and your father. He was sad when he lost them but he had you to raise, so he didn't dwell on the past."

Max still couldn't get used to someone reading his thoughts. He nodded. "What happened to my mother?"

"She left a note tucked in your blanket, handed you to her father, kissed him on the cheek, and vanished. That was the last anyone saw of her."

"What did the note say?" Max stared wide-eyed; how could his mother just leave him? All this time, he'd thought she had a terrible accident, but she'd chosen to leave him. His eyes clouded again; he had to choke back the urge to cry. He was too old to sit there and carry on as though he were a little child.

"We understand how you feel. Bigger men than you have sat here before me and cried for a lesser cause."

The Count's words didn't make Max feel any better. He didn't want these two important people in his life to see him blubber. He blinked steadily, swallowed hard, and repeated his question again in a cracked voice. "What did the note say?"

"It said she couldn't care for you because of her feelings of guilt and hopelessness. She asked your grandfather to take good care of you until she returned."

"But she didn't come back! Something must've happened to her. What happened, do you know?" Max's hopes dwindled under the look the Count gave him.

"We tried to find her, but we were never able to. It's as though she simply vanished. We always felt if she'd been captured and killed, her body would have been returned to us with an evil tale of her capture and demise."

"What about my grandfather? Where is he?"

Count Triad gave Max an unwavering look. "The vampires have him."

Max could feel his blood boil. His face grew hot with anger; then he realized the Count said they have him.

"That means he is still alive?"

Nodding, the Count leaned forward. "Yes, my boy, he's alive. And that's where you come in."

Max sat frozen. "I don't understand."

"Because you're the son of a very powerful man and a woman whose father was a lab experiment you are extremely powerful in your own right. Though your strength must be perfected and you have much to learn, you have the potential to be a great leader. The Vampires know that, they want to get you and teach you to their standards so that you would be a part of their world. They also would treat you as though you were a lab rat in order to find out how the Vamparians function."

Max watched incredulously as the story unfolded.

"The night you and your grandfather were taken from the farm was carefully planned; we actually set the plan into motion. We discovered that the Vampires found out you were living among the humans and we knew it would only be a matter of time before they arrived at your doorstep. You see, the farm you lived on was the headquarters for much of our work in the human world, and we couldn't let them find it and most importantly the two of you. Since the two of you were a big part of the human world there would be many questions from the humans and a lot of searching if we just had you transported out of there. So Ben, Dramid and I planned and arranged for the phone calls to the sheriff who is actually a Mediator for the Vamparians. We hoped that by making the move have a legitimate reason in the human world then the Vampires and who ever their spies were would not think anything of a story of a man gone insane and a boy taken away."

Max sat up his eyes open wide. "Sheriff Peters knows about you, or us, all of this?"

The Count nodded.

"Absolutely he is a Mediator, which means he is a human who knows all about Vampires and Vamparians. The Mediators contact us when a suspected case of Vampire crimes has occurred. Vampires, as you probably know, cause a lot of destruction and do a great deal of killing. There are many humans who have been witness to the viciousness; still others, of course are oblivious to anything implausible. There are those who wish to have our help, and of course we help them since our ability to determine who is a Vampire and who is not; is an extra perception that only we possess. The humans do not have that ability; therefore it is beneficial for them to sound off when they suspect that a vampire involved killing or abduction has taken place. When we are made aware of the incident we are very dedicated and skillful at our detective work, we find them and attack the perpetrators before they can inflict any further damage on the human world. We are also much more proficient at battling the Vampires."

The Count took a deep breath and a hearty swig of a thick clear liquid before continuing. "Okay back to the manner by which we got you out of there." The Count breathed a deep sigh. "Dramid would you like to continue this story for a moment and let me rest my tongue."

The Count smiled as Dramid picked up where he had left off. "We told several of the children's agencies and the newspapers that you may be in danger because your grandfather might be losing his mind. We indicated that Ben needed to be checked out by a professional. That way, the locals would talk about your grandfather having and needing some medical attention. I, of course, did not realize how preposterous the rumors would be."

"Nor did I." The Count added hastily.

Dramid nodded and continued. "Humans are hungry for any kind of scandal and many people jumped on that bandwagon with appalling stories of your abuse and neglect. It was really quite ridiculous.

We were sure that the story would buy us the time we needed to get the two of you here safely and satisfy the human curiosity all in one. We planned on transporting you both as soon as the rumors calmed and we could safely pull you out. It backfired; again someone double crossed us and told the Vampires where Ben was. They were unable to find you at the orphanage so we were at least lucky about that.

Beuffus stayed with Ben he disguised himself as a stray cat and was staying at the mental hospital to keep an eye on him. He became impatient when he realized that the Vampires were on their way to get Ben, and instead of waiting and discussing what we should do, he left with your grandfather and tried to come back here. He was found out and intercepted. Beuffus and Ben were caught. Fortunately, Beuffus escaped and was able to get back here and tell us what happened. They took Ben, but luckily you were safe at the orphanage." Dramid paused and cleared his throat.

The Count stared at the black raven in the glass viewer and said. "Beuffus's eagerness caused Ben to be captured. Beuffus was punished, although I feel his heart was in the right place.

Max's eyes widened also noticing Beuffus as the Black raven in the viewer, "that's why Beuffus is forced to be that bird now. Is that the mistake he made?"

Dramid looked up from his folded hands on the table and with a look towards the Count, he nodded. "Beuffus is a good Vamparian, loyal and honest; he just gets a bit headstrong sometimes and reacts without thinking."

"That's why he insisted Sam and Tracie come with me here." Max smiled; for that reason he was glad Beuffus was a little headstrong. "How long will Beuffus be punished for what he did? Gramps would not want him to remain sentenced as a bird for what occurred it could have happened to anyone."

"Due to Beuffus' rush on things, your grandfather was taken and remains a prisoner. You are correct though, I feel Beuffus has been punished long enough I will personally remove the spell." The Count appeared genuinely concerned about lifting Beuffus from his punishment.

Max smiled. "That will make Beuffus happy. Three years is a long time to be a bird even though he was only a bird when he was at the orphanage." Max said as he looked curiously at the Count. "Uh Sir why couldn't my Gramps use his powers to get away – or do you think they've— killed him by now?"

"Oh, no, they wouldn't kill him; he's one of the original experiments, and because the doctor had put a special curse on all of the fifty originals produced, they would not dare to kill one. They learned that the hard way when Bradicus Von Marriam was killed. After they killed him, the cells of his body came to life and, like a plague, became invisible killing forces which killed hundreds of the Vampires. The Vampires would like very much to figure out what that spell was and how it works. I am sure they are studying Ben's every move and blood cell."

"Why do they want me? I'm not a created original."

"No, you're much more valuable. You're a cross between the daughter of an original and a true vampire. You're what a leader is made of. They want to capture you young so they can train your mind."

"Train it for what?"

"To be their new leader, I fear. You see, they remember how strong and valuable your father was to them, when he was one of them. They'll hold your grandfather in front of you to get you to do their bidding until you're in so deep you can't get out." The Count paused and cleared his throat before continuing.

"We had to split you two up on purpose just in case they had discovered you both. At least until each was securely here because of that very reason. Capturing both of you would be disastrous. Unfortunately, Ben didn't make it here and, well, because we cannot risk losing you to them we must keep you where we know they would never suspect

"How are we going to save my grandfather? We can't just leave him there." Max said hopefully.

The Count nodded, "we just recently discovered where they may be keeping him. We'll know for sure soon."

"Why couldn't I just make myself known, say I'll trade myself for him, and then attack them when they come out? You said we're powerful."

"Yes, we are powerful, but we don't go looking for conflict. We protect ourselves and take care not to become exposed."

"If you're so powerful, why can't I stay here? I could learn to be stronger. I'll work hard and never complain." Max felt as though he was bargaining for his life, which he was.

"We'd love to have you here with us, but until your grandfather's returned or you are at the age where your powers are strong enough to protect yourself we can't risk it. You see, the attack that happened the other day was small. Others have been much bigger and lasted longer with many lives lost. If we let our guard down just once, you might be taken. If our wolves had not been doing a superior job the other day you may already have been discovered by the young spy who was found. Thankfully, they did their jobs. We can't risk letting them use your grandfather and you against one another. You can come for short visits, but you can't come permanently until you turn fifteen – and that's only if we've rescued your grandfather."

"FIFTEEN! That's a hundred years from now! I can't survive that orphanage for three more years. I just can't! They'll kill me. If not by food poisoning, they'll lock me up and throw away the key and I'll be nothing but a bone when you come for me." Max snorted and crossed his arms defiantly. "And besides, is that the best place you could find to keep me? You know its torture for me there."

The Count nodded, "That's why it's perfect. No one would ever suspect a descendant of your mother and father to be stuck in a dark hole like Crudder. Not only is it a ramshackle building but it is also the old home of one of the Vampires most horrific killers of all time Dracula's brother, Raducula the handsome. Because he had lived there and had carried out much of the carnage in that era he would never return to that place and time. In his twisted mind that place never existed. None of the other Vampires would disgrace Raducula by ever going near that place"

Max uncrossed his arms and flung himself forward while slapping both hands on the table. "Dracula's brother lived at Crudder orphanage where I now live?" Max asked disbelievingly.

"I am afraid so Max, he slept there by day and killed by night." Dramid watched Max closely.

Max cleared his throat as an unforgettable image of two small frightened children and a washed-out woman entered his mind. "Do you know if there was a Mrs. Raducula and two small kids that lived there with him?"

The Count nodded, "Indeed there was a woman and her children, however they were mostly ignored and later I believe they were executed by him or because of him."

Max grimaced. "Bailey thought that the strange things he had been witness to years ago may have been the ghosts of the two children. He said they were starved for attention and locked away and that their mother jumped out of the attic window and the father into the pond out back and was never seen again. So was Raducula the father of the children?"

The Count shook his head, "Actually the truth of the matter is that the family in which you are referring to, just happened to live happily in that home that is now Crudder orphanage. Unfortunately at some time Raducula saw the woman and decided he wanted her. The gentleman that you believe to have jumped into the pond was actually thrown from the top floor window. He landed unfortunately in a way that broke his neck and he died shortly after. The woman was spellbound by Raducula and became just an empty shell with not a thought in her head; she became in essence, a zombie that walked the nights. The woman's oldest child—a daughter became despondent after having been mentally abandoned by her mother for a cruel man and losing her father, she jumped out the top window and killed herself. The youngest child— a boy seemed to have vanished. Raducula is very charming and quite handsome, hence the name Raducula the Handsome. He is, however, a horrible soul and I fear that the actual events depicting the lives and deaths of the family are known only to them and to him." Count Triad leaned forward and took another swig from the glass in front of him.

Dramid cleared his throat and added, "Unfortunately the stories, and there have been many, are in fact stories. When the family started to die off one by one it was the imaginations and assumptions of the humans that began a large assortment of bizarre tales."

"And my dear boy," Count Triad said, "as for ghosts they do exist, but as to Bailey's suggestion of the children haunting that place, I do not know for sure. One would think they would find a far better place to— drift." The count shrugged having not been sure how to end the last statement. Not wanting to use the word haunt since he was certain these young children would not actually want to haunt any place.

Max nodded still wondering about the painting in Mr. Crater's office. "I saw a picture in Mr. Crater's office of an intimidating man a sad woman and two kids do you think that could have been them?"

Dramid nodded, "that is them. Several times I have wanted to remove that painting; however I was sure you or one of the others would be blamed for it, so I have left it. It seems that Raducula is your Mr. Craters role model, possibly due to the horrified look in the youngster's eyes and the evil look in Raducula's. I believe Mr. Crater would like to have all of you students looking at him with such horror in your eyes. Fortunately though he is quite mild in comparison to Raducula"

Max looked stunned. "I live in the same house as Dracula's awful hideous brother and there could be ghosts of mistreated children lurking around. This is the exact family of vampires that want me— and I live right under their noses, so to speak." Max sat back in the chair, his ashen face and wide eyes made the Count and Dramid think they may have revealed far too much information.

"Max, you have nothing to fear. You can be sure none of the Vampires would return to the orphanage looking for you, I assure you," The Count declared firmly. "It would be far more likely for them to look here or other similar places, not in the long forgotten home of misdeeds from many years ago."

Dramid spoke up with a gleam in his eye. "Listen Max we intend to help you a bit more than we have in the past. I told you that. We can make it more bearable."

"I just don't know how I can go back there after being here," Max groaned with a sadness in his voice. He was already missing this place as he recalled his miserable existence at the orphanage.

"You're strong, Max. You can do this; if not for yourself, but for us and your Grandpa Ben."

"This is your sacrifice; for the greater cause, you have to do this Max – for our people and yourself." Dramid reached over and squeezed his shoulder. There was an uncomfortable pause

"Beuffus and I will be there often, now that you know we exist we can spend more time helping you, and there is always someone here monitoring the viewer so if we can't be there in person we are just a shout away." Max thought about all the things that had happened, and he wondered how much they had already helped him.

"So just like the day in the library and that night in the English class, you can help me out of tight spots?"

Dramid nodded.

"And what about the day Rubin, Gorfus, and Lenny beat each other up? Was that you also?"

"You might say I gave them a little boost. You got them started. I just had to make sure the task was completed."

"Cool! So I am starting to get some powers?"

"From here on out, you'll see them getting stronger and stronger. We will need to get you back here so you can learn to perfect those powers. You also need to know it is important for you to be careful using your powers it could bring about unwanted attention." Max thought about it, what was the use of having powers if you couldn't turn Lenny into a warty old toad. The real question Max needed to know was. "When my grandpa gets back, I get to live back with him, don't I – back on the farm?" As he mentioned the farm, the viewer filled with a vision of the rolling green fields. Max sat up and looked deep into the glass viewer.

Dramid and the Count looked at each other and then back at Max. "No, that won't be possible. The farm will only be used for meetings in the human world. You were only there because your Grandfather wanted you to experience human tradition and behaviors. Naturally, he would have accompanied you here on your fifteenth birthday if we had not had this misfortune."

Max tried to hide his disappointment. "But you will let me know when Gramps is found, won't you. I'll be able to see him, won't I?"

"Yes, of course. Your grandfather lived here in this town for most of his life. It's just when he started to raise you that he wanted things as quiet and normal as possible until you reached the age of fifteen. Once he is found, he will return here, as will you." Dramid avowed firmly.

"Yes, my boy. In fact, we've been meeting on the subject of whether or not you can return here for visits. We feel it would be nice to have you here for Christmas vacation and a little while in the middle of the year, you have something called spring rest?" The Count raised his eyebrows awaiting a reply.

"Uh, it's called Spring break. We get three days of, well, no school work."

"At that time you possibly can spend those three days here," The Count smiled.

"Wow that would be great! Will Sam and Tracie get to come also?"

"I'm sorry, Max, but putting them in danger again is out of the question." Count Triad's gaze never wavered; Max was certain he meant what he had said.

"They're in danger every day of the week at that school. I don't see how much worse it could get. They're my best friends and they have nothing. At least I know I have you guys, this place, and my Gramps. They have nothing! Please! They won't blame you if something happens." Max pleaded.

"No, they won't blame us because there will be nothing left of them to do the blaming." The Count sighed. He took a deep breath and while he looked away from Max he mumbled. "We will think about it, and can discuss it further when the time comes." The Count could not bear to disappoint Max on his last days with them.

"We need to tell you we doubt it very much, but we will try. A higher council makes those decisions." Dramid declared.

The Count leaned back in his chair looking relieved that Max hadn't pursued the subject further. He smiled and said. "You know, there isn't much more to tell. Let's have a look into the glass here, and then you should go have some fun. You've only today and tomorrow left here."

For an hour or more, Max listened and gazed into the round glass ball that showed past and present. He saw his parents when they were younger. He saw battles – and much more. He could have watched for hours, but Dramid and the Count insisted that he needed fresh air and sunshine.

A Kid with a Grudge

CHAPTER EIGHTEEN

As Max left the room, a whole new batch of thoughts plagued his mind. He, Max Morgan, was a Vamparian, descended from Vampires? He'd always thought Vampires were fictional characters, not part of his bloodline. Wow! The place where Max lived, the cold building on Crudder Street was actually Dracula's Brothers house. His mind searched through the last thirteen years trying with much effort to make some sense out of what he had just learned. Preoccupied, he walked down the winding staircase and out into the cold sunshine. Standing there on the stone steps he pushed aside the morning's information determined to enjoy the rest of the day.

A flurry of activity filled the yard below. Max scanned the grounds for his friends. As he paused on the steps, Biff Duncan appeared and stood directly in front of him. Max moved left, then right. Biff stayed in front of him.

"What's your problem?" Max stood his ground, looking into the other boy's eyes. Biff was several inches shorter, since he was standing one step down.

Biff snarled at him. "Maybe you'd like to see just how splendid you really are. Want to have a go at it then?"

"A go at what?" Max asked.

"C'mon, I'll show you. But when I win and you get hurt, you can't go running and crying, telling on me. We'll just know who's the best and most powerful."

Max appeared confused. "What are you talking about the best and most powerful at what? I won't fight with you, if that's what you're talking about. You're of no interest to me; your problem is your problem, not mine." He stepped around Biff in an effort to leave. He wanted to spend the day having fun, not dealing with another wannabe bully. Max stepped forward, but his legs didn't cooperate they felt as though they had turned to rubber. He tried to keep from falling, but he flailed forward and landed on the grass below the steps. He picked himself up, his body aching from the impact.

What had happened to his legs? From the hysterical laughter behind him, he knew he need not look further. Max rose slowly and unsteadily, realizing Biff had made a spectacle of him. As other students gathered to investigate, one tall boy grabbed Max by the arm to steady him.

"There you go. Are you ok?"

"Yes, I think so. Thanks; I'm not sure what happened."

"I can promise you Biff had something to do with it," The tall kid motioned with his head in the direction of the laughter. Max noticed Biff was the only one laughing. He felt satisfied that these students weren't all a bunch of thoughtless sheep that followed someone else because they had no ability to think for themselves.

"He's someone you should stay away from in case you haven't already noticed. By the way, my name is Pete." Pete was very tall and slender his dark brown skin and black hair shown in contrast to his shining white teeth. His earth brown eyes surveyed Max as he swept away several strands of grass from Max's shoulder.

"I'm Max."

"I know who you are, I've wanted to take time to say hello, but with studies, valentia and all the activities, I've had a bit of trouble fitting you in. It's nice to finally meet you; I can handle this if you wish." He motioned toward Biff.

"No, I think I better handle it myself or he'll think he can get away with treating me this way."

Pete shrugged. "Oh, he'll do that anyway. He seems to think he's the best at everything."

"He may be, but I can't let him get away with it or I—" Max's words trailed off as he watched three large bats drag a yelling and kicking Biff up into the pale blue sky and away.

"What was that? Where did he go?"

Pete motioned to the stairs. There standing on the top step Beuffus, grinned a roguish grin. "You probably did not want me interfering, but I'm afraid I couldn't help myself. You see, he reminds me so much of your ornery little school chums, and I didn't want you to get hurt. Biff is an intermediate student – he's had two years of training where you've had none. Someday you'll be one of the best, but that will take time and maturity. The first lesson is that we don't fight with fellow students unless it's absolutely necessary. This was NOT one of those times."

Max nodded his agreement, "I just don't want it to be like at the orphanage; once they start picking on you they never stop."

"Anywhere you go in life, Max, there will be some sort of adversity. You have to overcome it, not necessarily by fighting or running, but by believing in yourself and not letting others define your self worth for you – especially the Biff's and Lenny's of the world." He motioned to the other students. "Now go have some fun with the others. Pete would probably like to meet your friends."

Max smiled. "Thanks, Beuffus. Hey, by the way, where did they take Biff?"

"That's for the bad kids to know and hopefully you to never find out. Unfortunately, he'll be back – but not before you leave."

Max and Pete walked off laughing at Beuffus who was just a kid at heart. Max spent the next several hours listening to Pete's tales of life in Transfellula. They sat outside on a stone hearth next to a crackling fire. Max was mesmerized by the stories of intrigue, excitement, and gory battles. He was amazed by Pete's intelligence and talent. Max enjoyed an incredible afternoon learning about a world he'd soon be part of.

While Max had been engrossed, Tracie and Sam actually tried a quick round of spider racing. Tracie was usually afraid of spiders; however these did not seem entirely spider- like. They were more like very large ugly dogs with eight legs and short itchy hair covering their long bodies. An oval track with obstacles, jumps and giant underground caverns made the races especially thrilling. Tracie found it tricky to stay astride as the spider scrambled over the jumps. Her mount seemed much rougher than the other nine spiders, the cuts and bruises where evidence of her lacking skill.

She soon learned that her two new friends were young and energetic. They kept her busy all afternoon with one thing or another. Sam had been particularly interested in a very attractive girl who was thrilled with the chance to learn about the human world and, in turn, she showed him some of the skills she had learned in her years at the school. When the evening air began to turn colder, a loud howl echoed through the chaos signaling the evening meal. In an instant, hungry students lined up and filed back into the warm castle. At the steps, Max met up with Sam and Tracie. "Hey, what have you been up to all day?" Tracie asked.

"I've been learning a lot about my family and this place; I don't think you'll believe it when I tell you. I'll have to explain it later, when we have more time."

"Did you learn anything about your Gramps?" Sam asked

"Oh, yeah, more then I could have imagined."

Sam and Tracie looked at Max with a question in their eyes, but he shook his head. "I'm telling you, we'll have to talk later. It's just way too hard to believe."

"If you say so," Sam shrugged. They bound up the steps into the dining area, retrieved their meals, and began eating hungrily. Max looked around the room, knowing it was almost time for them to leave – only a couple of days left. Thoroughly stuffing themselves, they dragged their tired bodies lethargically out of the dining room. After all the excitement of the day, Max just wanted to do nothing.

"Let's go up to the commons and lounge around for the rest of the evening," Tracie said.

Max yawned. "That sounds like a great idea. I was just thinking how tired I am. It would give us enough time for me to tell you all about my bizarre background," he offered. They made their way up the tangled pathways to the common room.

Tracie yawned and stretched. "Those two little kids about killed me today." She rubbed her stiff neck. "Of course, Casanova here spent most of his time with a tall, black- haired beauty." She quipped.

Sam cleared his throat and changed the subject. "Do you know they ride spiders here, and have dragon-spitting contests? And I'm not talking saliva; they spit big red fireballs— I did meet someone interesting. Her name is Saeleeze she's pretty cool," Sam grinned.

"Sleeze what kind of name is that?" Tracie joked.

"Its Saaa leeze, I said, not sleeze. You would like her Trace; she's pretty much a tomboy. Heck she was digging around in the dirt for these nasty mean little slug- like things that are called Globbers. They're ugly, red, squishy buggers with horns. They've got short arms with two clawed fingers, but no legs so they propel themselves by their rounded back ends. They would spit, bite and scratch her but she just kept digging them up. She said they were responsible for making people trip and fall. They wait until you walk by, then they jump up and grab your foot with their stubby arms. After she caught them she would shoot them out of the yard with a sling shot."

Tracie and Max stared dubiously at Sam. "Wow, sounds — entertaining to me," Tracie said mockingly.

Sam shrugged, "I thought it was."

Max smiled, thinking how much he'd miss his friends. It didn't seem they'd be able to come back with him, no matter how hard he tried to persuade the Count. They passed other students in the hallway, some going to their rooms, others headed for an indoor field to play more games. Some sat in the activity rooms looking at the glass viewers, apparently talking with loved ones.

Inside the commons, the three friends plopped down on one of the overstuffed couches in front of the fireplace. The warm fire glowed brightly, casting shadows on the orderly rows of books. Standing in the corner, a suit of armor seemed to dance as the shadows and light played off the shining metal exterior.

Max filled them in on all the details.

"YOU'RE A WHAT?" Tracie exclaimed. "DERIVED FROM WHAT?"

"I know things are strange here, but really Max— you a Vampire?" Sam stared frozen-faced at Max.

"Are you sure this isn't some sort of joke?" Tracie asked. "Let me see your teeth!" She stared at him closely.

"It's not like that, I'm only a form of a vampire not an actual one. Max said impaitiently.

They both stared at him in silence for several moments. Sam broke the silence, "you know, come to think of it, the vampire thing explains a lot of the weird stuff we've seen: flying dragons, bats, and people changing to other forms of life. Think about all the strange things these people think of as normal."

Max nodded, "My thoughts exactly. This is no joke; it's for real, and the best part is that I really don't belong in that orphanage. It's just a hideout for me right now."

Sam and Tracie looked at each other, trying to be happy for their friend. In reality, this news meant they didn't belong in Max's world.

He would soon be gone, lost to them forever. They each wondered what it would be like without him. They wished they had some sort of hidden past that would carry them away from the orphanage before their eighteenth birthdays.

Max watched his friends, knowing how hurt they felt – not because he was different, but because he couldn't include them in his world. In trying to make them feel better and to give them hope, he lied to his friends for the first time.

"Hey guys don't look so sad. I already asked if you could come back with me when it was safe, and they said they'll think about it. That means you'll probably be coming back with me."

Tracie clapped her hands. "Wow, you mean it, Max? That's great! It would be so cool to go to school here. I wonder what they teach, if its normal lessons or just bat and dragon stuff."

Her excited chatter escaped Max as he looked down at his hands fiddling with the fringe of the pillow on his lap. It was hard to look his friends in the eye. He'd just told a very big lie, and though it was a lie told with good intentions, that didn't make it much better. Nevertheless, sitting there in the room with the warm fire glowing and his friends nearby, Max felt happy. But he knew his happiness would soon end, because his return to the orphanage was imminent.

Tracie continued babbling. Her chatter finally cut through Max's thoughts "When do we have to leave to go back?" She asked for the third time.

"Way too soon is all I can say," Sam finally answered for Max.

"Yeah that's for sure." Max hesitated. "I was just wondering what Mrs. Rosenblam will think when she sees we've gained weight instead of lost."

"Yeah." Tracie smiled. She paused; picturing Mrs. Rosenblam then continued. "I'll bet her sour old face will really scrunch up when she sees us."

They stayed in the commons long into the night, just talking. No one bothered them, no one told them to get to bed. It was nice. They were served large bowls of a food called criffles, a deliciously crunchy sweet, yet salty snack food. Large mugs of ice cold fallot juice accompanied the snacks; it was brought to them on a tray carried by a tall, scary looking man dressed in a long gray cape. His quiet sudden entrance nearly scared Tracie to death, especially since Max had been telling them about the vampires and their grizzly contact with the humans that Pete had told him about. The man entered silently, the expression on his fearsome face never changed; he placed a tray on the table in front of them, nodded, and vanished through a door behind the bookcase. They watched in amazement, and then looked at each other, wondering if it was safe to eat the treats. Assuming that it was safe, they devoured them in record time.

Sometime after midnight, they decided to retire to the warmth of their beds.

The next morning, Max awoke to a stormy day; rain beat a tempo on the window. Far away in the distance a hazy mist rose off the valley. Max stood at the bedroom window and watched as the rain pelted down. The cold air seemed to find every crack in the stone castle. After three days of excitement, they welcomed the chance to laze around, play games, eat, nap and explore the castle. The rooms were silent, because most of the students had either gone home for the holiday or were attending an out -of -town valentia game. Some had gone to the town of Sparkwood to share in the local festivities.

The three of them were sitting around in the warm commons reading and resting when Tracie jumped up and went to her room. Sam and Tracie had not had the time to show Max their gifts since there had been more pressing subjects to discuss. This seemed like the perfect moment. She returned a few minutes later carrying the blue crystal necklace.

"This is by far the most interesting gift I have ever received." Tracie exclaimed holding up her necklace for Max to see along with the instructions for him to read. "Can you believe that I can actually create a person just by shining this in the mirror I haven't had time to try it yet, but it will be interesting. I don't know how I'll picture her but the instructions say however I picture her is how she'll be."

Max was speechless as he read the instructions and glanced at the sky blue charm dangling from the antique gold chain. "It's amazing alright. Will she have a name?"

Tracie's smile faded; "well of course she'll have a name, her name will be— Ciji." She spat.

"Okay then, you don't have to bite my head off." Max looked from Tracie to the necklace. "What's your problem anyway?" Max asked.

"I'm sorry; I'm just getting edgy the closer it gets to us having to leave this place."

Max nodded. "Yeah I know what you mean I feel the same way; we need to make the best of it though." Max said.

Sam took the cue and left the room, he returned a short time later with his ghost finder, he had spent a good part of the previous day looking at the ghosts that actually roamed around outside. He had not put the ghost finder to use inside since he was slightly uncomfortable about knowing if they actually roamed the halls.

"Here Max look at this." Sam handed Max the silver rimmed glasses and told him what they were.

Max quickly slid them onto his face, and they rested comfortably on his nose. "Are you serious? Oh, wow. Hey." Max pulled them off as quickly as he had put them on. "That was spooky. They're everywhere in here; as a matter of fact there's one on your lap right now."

Sam's eyes widened and he jumped to his feet. "I knew it; I knew it, I wasn't going to put these on in here, how creepy." He frantically brushed at his legs.

Tracie giggled. "The note said they wouldn't hurt you, so relax."

"Yeah, well, I still don't like knowing, especially if they're sitting on my lap." Sam swung his arms around as though punching the air.

They spent the next few hours discussing the gifts and finally convinced Sam to look at the ghosts and try to get them to converse. It was a perfect afternoon.

Max spent the last of the daylight hours just staring out into the vast countryside.

The storm outside the castle walls raged more violently as the dark of night moved in. Max shivered as he watched the wind bend the trees unnaturally.

The day came and went all too quickly and they slept well that night, warm and cozy, for the last time, before they would return to the hard miserable cots.

The Scene in the Viewer

CHAPTER NINETEEN

The early morning just before dawn was bitter cold. The sky was clear and the bluish- full moon cast a shimmering glow over the fresh white snow on the distant mountains. Max noticed how deserted the yard was as he stood at the window, peering out over the country. Tiny lights shone from the houses as smoke billowed out the chimneys. As he stared out at the distant village he couldn't help but wonder where all of the other students lived and where his Gramps and mother had lived when they had been here.

Max had so many questions and so little time. He had been cast through a whirlwind of oddities only to be thrown onto the banks of an even greater phenomenon. He was a vamparian he belonged here, this was his heritage. His immediate family was no longer available to give him the answers to his inquiries. On the other hand he vowed that he would get his answers, he was sure of that, at some point in time he would return to this magnificent place and he would ask all the questions and would not take "we will tell you later" as an answer. He would be alright he just needed to be patient.

He was engrossed by the view and soon daylight crept in. The grounds and the castle seemed almost deserted. Max scanned the yard and he noticed a wolf lurking around the perimeter, while above him several bats circled the sky. A long-legged, rotund, black cat Max recognized as the Count's stalked through the yard, sneaking up on —he wasn't exactly sure what. At this distance, he could just barely make out what the cat had in its sights. They were cherry red against the yellow grass, and their horns poked out of their heads and waggled around as they propelled themselves away from the cat. Max thought of Sam and his story of the Globbers that Saeleeze had flung out of the yard. Max wondered what the cat intended on doing with them were he to catch one. He shrugged and turned away from the window. Sam lay silently in his bed, still asleep. His steady breathing was the only sound in the room. Max sat in a soft chair next to the window and returned his gaze out over the country. He was still trying to make sense of all he'd learned these past few days. A heavy feeling of sadness came over him as he realized they'd be leaving today.

He belonged here; he was a part of this place. If only he could find his Gramps so they could both be safe. He wondered if there was any way that he could pinpoint Gramps' location. After all, this would be his last day here – and his last chance to investigate.

He jumped up and went over to the table next to his bed, where he'd left his viewer the night before. Excited, he sat back in the chair, wondering if he could find some sort of clue in the viewer. All he had to do was put his hands on the small glass stone, peer into it, and concentrate on a particular person, place, or thing in the castle.

Time passed, Max concentrated hard, his eyes ached from staring into the stone. Suddenly Count Triad appeared in such lifelike form that Max wanted to wish him good morning. Although it took an advanced viewer to give out sound along with the picture, Max could hone in close enough to view the stack of papers on the Counts desk. He could see a note that the Count was reading, staring hard at the paper on the Count's desk. He read:

Dear Count,

We have been a long time in trying to discover the whereabouts of your friend and colleague Benjamin Morgan. We do believe he is being held in the Graylock Castle in Quintella Forest near Water's Edge. We await your instructions as to whether or not to proceed.

A shiver ran up Max's spine. They'd found his grandfather; now they could save him. He watched as Count Triad sat back in his chair and turned the letter over, and then looked up – as if he could tell someone was watching. Max felt startled to be caught eavesdropping. He released the viewer as if it were hot.

Sitting back, Max felt as though he had betrayed the Count. He'd spied on him. What would the Count think of him?

"That's it, I'm going to go find out about Gramps. I have every right to know," he mumbled as he dressed. After washing up, he looked over at his sleeping friend. They'd been up very late; no harm in letting Sam sleep a bit longer.

He hurried out the door and down the hall, where Brugo knelt on the floor talking to a small orange mouse. "C'mon then, critter, you don't belong in this section of the castle. I'll take you to your friends if you just hop up here in my hand." To Max's surprise, the mouse jumped up into Brugo's hand. The big man gently stroked the mouse with a finger so large it hid the animal. Max watched curiously. Brugo had his back to him as he stood.

"Hello Max, how are ya doing this fine morning?"

"How did you? Never mind. I'm fine, I guess. Is there really a place for that mouse?"

"Sure there is. Only the orange and green ones though they catch and eat all the wingclipper bugs. These critters are good to have around. The wingclipper, however, are horrible nasty creatures. If they bite ya, welts the size of a mountain will appear and itch, you'll scratch yourself senseless. In fact, if you get a bed full of them, you'll be sorry enough to jump in the murky depths of Locksley's home out front."

"Well then, I'm glad you're taking him back to eat those, uh, wingclipper bugs."

"Yes sir, that's for sure. Let's go, feller." Brugo lumbered down the hall.

Max turned the other way and headed toward the main entrance. He needed to find the Count. The halls were deserted. As Max entered the adjoining room to the Count's office, a short, chubby creature scurried around behind a wooden barrel. The barrel held a variety of weapons. Max was curious as to what had ducked behind there. He walked around to find a pair of black, beady eyes staring out from behind the barrel.

"It's impolite to stare, you know." The squeaky voice was matter-of-fact and very curt.

"I'm sorry. I just saw you duck behind here and wanted to see what it was."

"Well I am certainly not an it. And who I am is none of your concern, so go on about your own business and leave me to mine." The creature made a hiss noise like that of a cornered cat. His thin top lip lifted defiantly revealing a massive assortment of pointy sharp teeth. Max felt a repulsed shock. He tried hard to recover the horrified look on his face in order to give this creature the respect he was demanding.

Max's forced smile now lingered somewhere at the corner of his mouth, "Uh—well okay, fine. I meant no harm. My name is Max by the way, and it was nice meeting you." Max would have extended his hand yet he was still concerned about all those teeth. After all, the strange thing might think he was offering his hand as a snack.

The creature closed his lips covering the white daggers and said. "Krymphus is my name. I work here." He then scurried off through a door beneath the wall. Max thought about how odd Krymphus was, of course the teeth had been the kicker, they looked downright evil. They didn't seem to belong to his plump body and face, with the donkey like ears, and tiny black eyes. The attitude though— irrefutably matched the teeth.

Max continued on his quest to find the Count. At the door of the Count's office, the tall, spooky guy from the night before stopped Max. "What can I do for you?" He asked in a deep, almost menacing voice.

"I, uh well, I need to talk to the Count if I could, please."

"You NEED to? What is the emergency? The Count's busy right now and wishes NOT to be disturbed."

"It's very important that I see him. Could you just ask him if he'll see me? My name is Max, Max Morgan."

"Very well. You stay here, I will check." The gruff man disappeared behind the door with a slam. What seemed a long time later he returned, wearing a look of disdain. "You can go in. Just keep the noise down."

"Thank you." Max walked through the door, glancing back at the man as he entered. He could feel dislike as the dark eyes burned holes into his back. It gave Max an uneasy feeling.

The room was quiet, not nearly as much activity as he'd seen on previous visits to the office. The Count looked up from slipping a note into a gold locket that hung around a bats' neck. He gave Max a warm welcome. "Max my boy, how nice to see you. I was just now thinking of the best way to get you safely back to that school of yours." The Count motioned to the bat. "I also have a message that I am sending out, but of course you already know that a reply is being awaited."

Max got right to the point. "I was just looking into my viewer and I —saw your letter. I didn't mean to spy, it just sort of happened."

The Count nodded. "It's nice to have such an advanced student with the concentration to connect on the other end of the viewer. Especially since you have had no training, your skills impress me. You weren't doing anything wrong by looking at my letter. I have to make some important decisions and involving you wasn't my intention."

"But I am involved. This is my Gramps we are talking about; he'd want me to know!"

"Actually, no, he would not. That's why he never told you any of this, because of your age. He also wouldn't want to endanger our way of life or your life. And certainly he wouldn't want us to take off trying to save him without being sure we could get the job done."

Thinking hard, Max knew the Count was right. His Gramps was always concerned about others first. Max looked at the floor. "I guess you're right, but what will you do? What does your response say?" Max motioned to the small bat awaiting his flight plan.

"This note will give permission to check further. We have to make sure this is legitimate and safe enough to pursue without losing several men in battle. You understand that, don't you?"

Max hung his head, disappointed. "Yeah, I guess."

"Now, then, we must get you something to eat and get ready to take you back to the orphanage. I'm sure they'll be looking for you three to be safely locked away when they open the door to that dark room." The Count glanced into one of the viewers. "We have less then eight hours to get you back. It's barely midnight right now at Crudder."

"I wish I could stay," Max murmured.

"Soon you'll be here for good, but for now we must go." The Count stood and carried the bat over to an open window. He uttered a few short sentences then let him fly out into the cold icy air.

Turning, he led Max out of the office. Conversation was light as they walked swiftly to the dining area. No one was around, the meal, as usual, was supreme.

Count Triad left Max so he could go consult with Dramid. Before the Count left, he told Max he'd send someone for Sam and Tracie.

A very tall, ebony haired woman with a flowing gray cape came forward. In her petite hands with eerily long fingernails she held a plate of food. "We have very few students here today so we won't be filling the hearth. Do let me know if you wish for more." She sat his plate down and left. Max enjoyed the silence of his breakfast. He ate slowly, trying to savor the moment.

Shortly after he finished, Sam and Tracie entered the dining area. "Hey Max, I didn't hear you leave this morning, what have you been up to this early?"

"I came down to talk with the Count." Max wasn't sure why but he didn't wish to get into the debate over his Gramps' looming rescue so he changed the subject. "It's sure quiet around here."

Sam nodded as the same woman approached carrying two heaping plates and setting them on the table with a cool nod.

"Thanks," Tracie uttered. The moment they had all dreaded was nearing. They sat in silence, while contemplating the journey back to the dreaded orphanage.

Departure

CHAPTER TWENTY

Dramid and Beuffus entered the room as the three were finishing. "Train's awaiting, kids. I know that's not a real pleasant thought, it's been nice to have you here," Beuffus said."

Dramid grasped Max's shoulder. "You three go get your stuff ready. We'll meet you at the front door in half an hour."

With their borrowed capes and clothes folded neatly on their beds, and wearing the outfits they'd arrived in, they were now ready to go. The three took one final look around.

"I'm sure going to miss this place." Tracie said as they strolled down the hall.

"Springs not to far off, we'll get to come back then." Max smiled. But the smile faded, as inwardly he was thinking he would return, but probably not them.

Half an hour later, they stood at the front door with Count Triad, Dramid, and Beuffus.

Smiling, the Count said. "It has been my pleasure to have you here for this short visit. We'll keep in touch. You have your viewer and I know you know how to use it."

With a meek smile, Max nodded. "Thanks for everything. We had fun. Let me know anything new about Gramps."

"I shall." Turning to Max's friends, the Count added. "Tracie and Sam, you two have been a delight. It was a pleasure meeting you. Take care."

With the farewells out of the way, the Count turned and walked back up the long stairway while the rest of them walked out of the castle.

Dramid looked down at Max and tried to lighten the mood. "We'll be leaving by a different means of transportation this time. We need to keep anyone from spotting us, and since its daylight they could hardly miss a flying dragon."

"How will we get there?" Max asked.

"You'll see."

They walked across the grounds and over the bridge that lay open, crossing the murky waters below that now lay crusted over with ice. It was a dismal morning; their heads couldn't have hung lower.

A loud rumble came from the direction of the forest near the same area where they'd landed five days earlier. Pulling up next to them on the road stood two huge, shining black horses. They stomped in place impatiently. A covered coach was hooked behind them and the door stood open.

"Climb in and take a seat." Dramid motioned them into the red velvet interior. Max looked up at the empty seat above the coach that should have held a driver. As they all stepped inside and sat down Max began to wonder who was driving. The coach jolted forward and then sped off down the dirt road.

Dramid looked at Max and smiled. "No one, these horses will get us where we are going because they know what we want." Max raised one eyebrow and sat quietly.

They entered the outskirts of town. There, across from an open field, stood a rustic building with a long platform stretching the full length of it. Several people were milling around it, some standing and talking, others hurrying along with baggage and boxes in tow. The horses came to a halt next to an antique looking train that was being loaded.

"We will take the train to Broiler's Pond." Dramid said to no one in particular.

Climbing down out of the coach Max instinctively looked up just to make sure no one had driven. The horses pawed and snorted impatiently. As their party climbed the steps of the platform the horses bolted off down the road, back in the direction of the castle. Max watched until it was out of sight, wishing he had stayed in the coach.

Standing there on the platform Max turned his attention to all of the people hurrying around. Most of the people greeted Dramid and Beuffus with warm welcomes and good wishes. Each time, Dramid simply nodded, while Beuffus struck up a short conversation.

They made there way to a groaning antique train and stood next to it waiting to board.

"Does this thing actually run?" Max asked a bit surprised looking at the ancient train. He wondered if they would be able to make it out of town in the old thing.

The engineer overheard Max and he chuckled. He gave the train a solid pat as though it were a living thing. "Don't let the looks fool you boy, this ol heap runs better then any of em on the tracks today, it'll make yer eyes water if ya stand outside when it's a movin."

Max nodded as the five of them entered the train. Inside, he found a roomy dining car filled with tables and chairs. Other cars had seats that were soft and comfy. A good-looking blond man greeted them; his blue-green eyes gazed into each of their faces. "You'll sit here." Holding his hand out, he motioned to a rounded bench seat where they would face one another on the journey. He carried a long dagger in a sheath on his left hip and on his right hip, he wore a sword. Through his dark warrior clothing, they could tell he was built solidly. "My name's Mason and I'll be your guard. This is Antonio, who'll assist me."

The other man nodded in their direction. He was a good head shorter than Mason, with dark hair, dark complexion and hazel eyes. His clean-cut appearance and hushed manner indicated he was much quieter than his comrade. Max thought they looked capable of handling any situation. His weapons included a strange-looking two-sided ax and short-bladed sword like a rapier. Both men were serious, no nonsense.

As the train pulled out of the station, the two guards faced the entrance doors with their backs to the five travelers. The unsteady rocking motion of the train would have made most people scurry for stability. Their balance was impeccable.

Max's inquisitive eyes traveled over the two men. "What exactly are they protecting us from?"

Dramid met his eyes with a steady gaze. "It's not the question of what – it's who. As I told you, many of the other kind want you, and they'll stop at nothing to get you."

"They'd actually come here to get me? It's not dark. I thought they could only come out in the dark?"

"Oh yes, they would do just about anything to get you." Beuffus said.

Dramid looked at Beuffus then back at Max and said. "The Vampires can only come out in the dark, but they have many evil creations working for them, as well as some humans looking to make an extra trinket or two."

"But we're in good hands. These two are experts. You can relax and let them take care of things." Beuffus grinned allowing his confidence to show.

"Are we riding this train all the way back to the school?" Tracie asked.

Dramid sat back and looked out the window answering calmly. "It should take four hours before we reach Broiler's Pond, an entryway into many destinations."

"Do we take a boat?" Tracie quizzed.

Beuffus grinned. "Not exactly." Beuffus answered, he had sensed Dramid's need for quiet concentration in order to keep a watchful eye for trouble. "You'll see. You wouldn't believe me if I told you, so just be patient." He added.

The train clamored down the tracks, making a lulling sound that made them want to lay back and rest. Yet watching the scenery outside was much more engaging. The snow-capped mountains with frozen waterfalls made Max instinctively pull his sweater tighter around his neck.

A few hours later, lunch was served. They devoured the sandwiches and the thick nectar type juice as though they hadn't eaten all day. All the while under the ever watchful eyes of their protectors and their guards who had no time to eat.

As the train neared its destination, a huge body of water came into view; the icy shoreline glistening in the sunlight. The train was suddenly swallowed up in darkness as it descended into a cave. The three unknowing passengers grabbed the edges of their seats. Sensing their fear, the guard named Mason turned to them. "Don't worry. We'll be traveling in darkness for awhile – we're headed for the bottom of the lake."

Max felt a bit more at ease. He asked Dramid "Have you been on this train before?"

"Yes I have. I just neglected to realize it might be daunting the first time."

"Yeah, just a little." Max agreed.

As the train slowed, a faint light appeared in the dark windows. The two guards became more alert and unsheathed their weapons.

Before Max could begin worrying, Beuffus and Dramid suddenly threw him onto the floor. Seconds later, Sam and Tracie joined him.

"Don't move," Dramid ordered.

Max laid flat, his face pressed against the stained smelly carpet. Bright streaks of light blasted his eyes momentarily blinding him. Rapidly he blinked until his sight returned. It all happened so fast, he didn't have time to ask questions – not that he'd dare. Loud screams filled the car and Max felt the train slam to a halt. He heard the screams and saw more flashes of light from within the train, then angry shouts and crashing.

The protectors moved forward into the path of three of the ugliest creatures Max had ever seen. Walking upright like men, they looked – and smelled – as though they'd been dead for many years. Their lanky bodies were hidden under flowing green robes. The faces looked like molten lava. Tracie whimpered and scooted closer to the wall; Max and Sam did likewise. By craning his neck, Max found he could watch the action without being seen.

The protectors sprang into action. Knives flew, swords sliced. The rotting arm belonging to one of the fierce creatures landed within a few feet of Max's face. As it lay there, the hand began to pull the severed arm towards Max who scooted deeper under the bench. Swiftly, Mason stepped over and kicked the arm away from Max's face. A short time later— which seemed like hours, the body parts of the green things lay scattered on the floor, still moving. Dramid and Beuffus roughly yanked Max, Tracie, and Sam up from the floor.

"Come on," Beuffus ordered.

"Don't look at or touch anything on the floor. Walk in line and follow Beuffus." Mason ordered.

"What are those things?" Max looked down at the pieces as they walked past.

Dramid shoved him from behind. "Never mind! You were told not to look. We need to get going. I'll tell you—"

Max finished the sentence for him—"later."

"Yeah," Dramid said.

They exited the train as flurries of people were still talking about the episode with the evil looking things that had stalked through the train. An older woman sat on a nearby bench trying to catch her breath, the conductor was fanning her with a stack of papers. "I was just so frightened I—I faint a lot you see— I." Beuffus strolled up to the woman and rested his hand on her shoulder. He then turned and strode back to the group. Max watched in amazement as the woman's ashen color changed to a light pink and she smiled, grabbed her bags and bustled away leaving the bewildered conductor staring after her.

"What did you just do to that woman?" Max whispered as he returned.

"Oh, I just cleared her mind of the incident. I find no reason for her to be that upset. It won't do her or anyone else any good." Max nodded as Beuffus smiled.

The protectors who had been conversing with Dramid now walked off ahead. Dramid ordered Max, Sam and Tracie to follow; they were led from the lighted platform into a dark tunnel. Dramid and Beuffus walked behind, still on the lookout.

Deep inside the tunnel Mason stopped, he pointed to a passageway leading off to the right. "This is where we leave you. You'll be fine from here on. Take care of yourselves." Within a split second, both men were gone, vanishing into the darkness.

"That was awesome; they were so cool," Tracie said dreamily.

Max and Sam rolled their eyes, mocking her. "They were soo cooool," Sam squeaked. The boys laughed.

Tracie shook her head. "You two are just jealous."

"Ha, not hardly!" Max grumped.

The passageway was narrowing and the rushing sound of water grew so loud that Max could hardly hear Tracie's surly reply. Sam however put in his two more cents. The grumbling continued and the pathway narrowed to single file.

Abruptly ending the bickering Dramid said, "Okay now, Beuffus will go first. You three follow. I'll be behind you. Don't be afraid. You'll need to hold your breath for the first few seconds when you feel water on your face. Then the swirling will pull it away so you can breathe. The entire journey takes fifteen minutes or so, but it will seem like only a few minutes. Just relax. We'll all meet up shortly."

Beuffus climbed a rickety ladder in front of him, and was sucked into the swirling water followed by Max who could hear nothing now except for the rushing water from the top of the ladder, just two steps away. He hesitated took a deep breathe and hesitated even longer. Suddenly Beuffus's hand reached out from the churning water and grabbed Max giving him a quick jerk. Max was startled and nearly forgot to hold his breath when suddenly just as Dramid had said, the water was pulled away from his face and he took a deep gulp of air into his lungs. All he could see around him was an intense blue-green swirl moving so fast it was nearly still. He'd had a dream just like this before—of being sucked down a huge culvert. That's what he thought it would feel like. Before he had time to be afraid, he was suddenly cast onto the ground feeling as though he had been hurled from a sling shot.

Beuffus was there standing before him with a childlike grin on his face. "I thought you were going to chicken out on me so I had to give you a little yank, sorry about that."

"It's okay; I wasn't so sure I was going to be able to make myself take the last step."

"Ah you would have done just fine. I just figured you needed a bit of a tug that's all."

Just as Max began to wonder, Tracie was thrown from the water as though she were spit out by a large fish. Sam, then Dramid followed.

Looking around, Max realized they were standing beside the creepy pond behind the orphanage. His gaze took in the depressing surroundings and the raggedy building. His heart sunk to his toes, he was back at the horrendous place he was forced to live in.

An entirely new thought scurried around in his brain, it was the fact that a fierce Vampire once lived here. His view of the place was now totally different. He thought of the sinister man in the painting. He looked at his hands. One question he had forgotten to ask was why the gloves in his heritage box, the hand shake with the Count, and touching the painting on the wall in Craters office had all produced the same electrical feeling. "Dramid" Max began hesitantly, "uh, well oh never mind I'll talk to you later. Won't I?"

"Of course you will, we can talk later but for now—"

Dramid's hand swept the air above the sopping wet trio; the water that soaked their clothes was gone.

"Come on, we don't want to be seen," Dramid whispered.

Walking behind the dead brush, they crouched low and headed for the familiar brick building. Standing outside the unsightly building; Max's stomach did a flip flop as he felt anxiety about the inevitable.

Dramid lifted his hand and pointed to the wall. "Go ahead."

They hesitated, so Beuffus went first – walking through the cement wall. Max followed, then the rest of them.

A horrible smell greeted them. Rotting food someone had thrown inside the room lay uneaten on the floor. Dramid waved his hand and the plates were clean. "There! Now they'll think you actually ate their vile food."

Beuffus turned to leave, and then paused.

"Okay, kids, we have to get out of here and figure out an appropriate disguise. Oh, and by the way Max, thanks for the good word, did you notice I'm no longer forced to wear feathers." He grinned, "We'll see you when you get out, which should be any moment." He and Dramid walked back through the wall.

Max, Tracie, and Sam stood in the darkness. A key clinked in the lock and the door swung opened. Light from the other room filtered in.

There stood Mrs. Rosenblam her lizard like face set in a sour expression.

Printed in the United States
62264LVS00004B/241-309